FRED SABERHAGEN

A jester by his efforts may give laughter to others, but by no labor can he seize it for himself.

I have touched minds that worked hard at revelry. Men and women who poured time and wealth and genius into costumes and music and smiling masks, seeking escape from the terror of the world . . . but who found no laughter.

And no escape.

BERSERKER ATTACK

Copyright © 1987 by Fred Saberhagen

MASQUE OF THE RED SHIFT and IN THE TEMPLE OF MARS copyright © 1965, 1966 by Galaxy Publishing Corporation.

BROTHER BERSERKER copyright © 1969 by Fred Saberhagen.

SMASHER copyright © 1978 by Mercury Press Inc.

Reprinted by arrangement with Tor Books

Printed in the United States of America

CONTENTS

INTRODUCTION

I, Third Historian of the Carmpan race, in gratitude to the Earth-descended race for their defense of my world, set down here for them my fragmentary vision of these battles from their great war against our common enemy.

The vision has been formed piece by piece through my contacts in past and present time with the minds of men and of machines. In these minds alien to me I often perceive what I cannot understand, yet what I see is true. And so I have truly set down the acts and words of Earth-descended men great and small and ordinary, the words and even the secret thoughts of your heroes and your traitors.

Looking into the past I have seen how in the twentieth century of your Christian calendar your forefathers on Earth first built radio detectors capable of sounding the deeps of interstellar space. On the day when whispers in our alien voices were first detected, straying in across the enormous intervals, the universe of stars became real to all Earth's nations and all her tribes.

They became aware of the real world surrounding them—a universe strange and immense beyond thought, possibly hostile, surrounding and shrinking all Earthmen alike. Like island savages just become aware of the great powers existing on and beyond their ocean, your nations began— sullenly, mistrustfully, almost against their will—to put aside their quarrels with one another.

In the same century the men of old Earth took their first steps into space. They studied our alien voices whenever *they could hear us. And when the men of old Earth began to travel faster than light, they followed our voices to seek us out.*

Your race and mine studied each other with eager science and with great caution and courtesy. We Carmpan and our older friends are more passive than you. We live in different environments and think mainly in different directions. We posed no threat to Earth. We saw to it that Earthmen were not crowded by our presence; physically and mentally they had to stretch to touch us. Ours, all the skills of keeping peace. Alas, for the day unthinkable that was to come, the day when we wished ourselves warlike!

You of Earth found uninhabited planets, where you could thrive in the warmth of suns much like your own. In large colonies and small you scattered yourselves across one segment of one arm of our slow-turning galaxy. To your settlers and frontiersmen the galaxy began to seem a friendly place, rich in worlds hanging ripe for your peaceful occupation.

The alien immensity surrounding you appeared to be not hostile after all. Imagined threats had receded behind horizons of silence and vastness. And so once more you allowed among yourselves the luxury of dangerous conflict, carrying the threat of suicidal violence.

No enforceable law existed among the planets. On each of your scattered colonies individual leaders maneuvered for personal power, distracting their people with real or imagined dangers posed by other Earth-descended men.

All further exploration was delayed, in the very days when the new and inexplicable radio voices were first heard drifting in from beyond your frontiers, the strange soon-to-be-terrible voices that conversed only in mathematics. Earth and Earth's colonies were divided each against all by suspicion, and in mutual fear were rapidly training and arming for war.

And at this point the very readiness for violence that had sometimes so nearly destroyed you, proved to be the means of life's survival. To us, the Carmpan watchers, the withdrawn seers and touchers of minds, it appeared that you had carried the crushing weight of war through all your history knowing that it would at last be needed, that this hour would strike when nothing less awful would serve.

When the hour struck and our enemy came without warning, you were ready with swarming battle-fleets. You were dispersed and dug in on scores of planets, and heavily armed. Because you were, some of you and some of us are now alive.

Not all our Carmpan psychology, our logic and vision and subtlety, would have availed us anything. The skills of peace and tolerance were useless, for our enemy was not alive.

What is thought, that mechanism seems to bring it forth?

MASQUE OF THE RED SHIFT

FINDING HIMSELF ALONE AND UNOCCUPIED, FELIPE NOGARA chose to spend a free moment in looking at the thing that had brought him out here beyond the last fringe of the galaxy. From the luxury of his quarters he stepped up into his private observation bubble. There, in a raised dome of invisible glass, he seemed to be standing outside the hull of his flagship *Nirvana*.

Under that hull, "below" the *Nirvana*'s artificial gravity, there slanted the bright disk of the galaxy, including in one of its arms all the star systems the Earth-descended man had yet explored. But in whatever direction Nogara looked, bright spots and points of light were plentiful. They were other galaxies, marching away at their recessional velocities of tens of thousands of miles per second, marching on out to the optical horizon of the universe.

Nogara had not come here to look at galaxies, however; he had come to look at something new, at a phenomenon never before seen by men at such close range.

It was made visible to him by the apparent pinching-together of the galaxies beyond it, and by the clouds and streamers of dust cascading into it. The star that formed the center of the phenomenon was itself held beyond human sight by the strength of its own gravity. Its mass, perhaps a billion times that of Sol, so bent spacetime around itself that not a photon of light could escape it with a visible wavelength.

The dusty debris of deep space tumbled and churned, falling into the grip of the hypermass. The falling dust built up static charges until lightning turned it into lumi-

1

nescent thunderclouds, and the flicker of the vast lightning shifted into the red before it vanished, near the bottom of the gravitational hill. Probably not even a neutrino could escape this sun. And no ship would dare approach much closer than *Nirvana* now rode.

Nogara had come out here to judge for himself if the recently discovered phenomenon might soon present any danger to inhabited planets; ordinary suns would go down like chips of wood into a whirlpool if the hypermass found them in its path. But it seemed that another thousand years would pass before any planets had to be evacuated; and before then the hypermass might have gorged itself on dust until its core imploded, whereupon most of its substance could be expected to reenter the universe in a most spectacular but less dangerous form.

Anyway, in another thousand years, it would be someone else's problem. Right now it might be said to be Nogara's—for men said that he ran the galaxy, if they said it of anyone.

A communicator sounded, calling him back to the enclosed luxury of his quarters, and he walked down quickly, glad of a reason to get out from under the galaxies.

He touched a plate with one finger. "What is it?"

"My lord, a courier ship has arrived. From the Flamland system. They are bringing . . ."

"Speak plainly. They are bringing my brother's body?"

"Yes, my lord. The launch bearing the coffin is already approaching *Nirvana*."

"I will meet the courier captain, alone, in the Great Hall. I want no ceremony. Have the robots at the airlock test the escort and the outside of the coffin for infection."

"Yes, my lord."

The mention of disease was a bit of misdirection. It was not the Flamland plague that had put Johann Karlsen into a box, though that was the official story. The doctors were supposed to have frozen the hero of the Stone Place as a last resort, to prevent his irreversible death.

An official lie was necessary because not even High Lord Nogara could lightly put out of the way the one man who had made the difference at the Stone Place. Since that battle it seemed that life in the galaxy would survive, though the fighting against the berserkers was still bitter.

The Great Hall was where Nogara met daily for feasting and pleasure with the forty or fifty people who were with him on *Nirvana*, as aides or crewmen or entertainers. But when he entered the Hall now he found it empty, save for one man who stood at attention beside a coffin.

Johann Karlsen's body and whatever remained of his life were sealed under the glass top of the heavy casket, which contained its own refrigeration and revival systems, controlled by a fiber-optic key theoretically impossible to duplicate. This key Nogara now demanded, with a gesture, from the courier captain.

The captain had the key hung around his neck, and it took him a moment to pull the golden chain over his head and hand it to Nogara. It was another moment before he remembered to bow; he was a spaceman and not a courtier. Nogara ignored the lapse of courtesy; it was his governors and admirals who were reinstituting ceremonies of rank; he himself cared nothing about how subordinates gestured and postured, so long as they obeyed intelligently.

Only now, with the key in his own hand, did Nogara look down at his frozen half-brother. The plotting doctors had shaved away Johann's short beard and his hair. His lips were marble pale, and his sightless open eyes were ice. But still the face above the folds of the draped and frozen sheet was undoubtedly Johann's. There was something that would not freeze.

"Leave me for a time," Nogara said. He turned to face the end of the Great Hall and waited, looking out through the wide viewport to where the hypermass blurred space like a bad lens.

When he heard the door ease shut behind the courier captain he turned back—and found himself facing the short figure of Oliver Mical, the man he had selected to replace Johann as governor of Flamland. Mical must have entered as the spaceman left, which Nogara thought might be taken as symbolic of something.

Resting his hand familiarly on the coffin, Mical raised one graying eyebrow in his habitual expression of weary amusement. His rather puffy face twitched in an overcivilized smile.

"How does Browning's line go?" Mical mused, glancing down at Karlsen. " 'Doing the king's work all the dim day long'—and now, this reward of virtue."

"Leave me," said Nogara.

Mical was in on the plot, as was hardly anyone else except the Flamland doctors. "I thought it best to appear to share your grief," he said. Then he looked at Nogara and ceased to argue. He made a bow that was mild mockery when the two of them were alone, and walked briskly to the door. Again it closed.

So, Johann. If you had plotted against me, I would have had you killed outright. But you were never a plotter, it was just that you served me too successfully, my enemies and friends alike began to love you too well. So here you are, my frozen conscience, the last conscience I'll ever have. Sooner or later you would have become ambitious, so it was either do this to you or kill you.

Now I'll put you away safely, and maybe someday you'll have another chance at life. It's a strange thought that someday you may stand musing over my coffin as I now stand over yours. No doubt you'll pray for what you think is my soul. . . . I can't do that for you, but I wish you sweet dreams. Dream of your Believers' heaven, not of your hell.

Nogara imagined a brain at absolute zero, its neurons superconducting, repeating one dream on and on and on. But that was nonsense.

"I cannot risk my power, Johann." This time he whispered the words aloud. "It was either this or have you killed." He turned again to the wide viewport.

"I suppose Thirty-three's gotten the body to Nogara already," said the Second Officer of Esteeler Courier Thirty-four, looking at the bridge chronometer. "It must be nice to declare yourself an emperor or whatever, and have people hurl themselves all over the galaxy to do everything for you."

"Can't be nice to have someone bring you your brother's corpse," said Captain Thurman Holt, studying his astrogational sphere. His ship's C-plus drive was rapidly stretching a lot of timelike interval between itself and the Flamland system. Even if Holt was not enthusiastic about his mission, he was glad to be away from Flamland, where Mical's political police were taking over.

"I wonder," said the Second, and chuckled.

"What's that mean?"

The Second looked over both shoulders, out of habit formed on Flamland. "Have you heard this one?" he asked. "Nogara is God—but half of his spacemen are atheists."

Holt smiled, but only faintly. "He's no mad tyrant, you know. Esteel's not the worst-run government in the galaxy. Nice guys don't put down rebellions."

"Karlsen did all right."

"That's right, he did."

The Second grimaced. "Oh, sure, Nogara could be worse, if you want to be serious about it. He's a politician.

But I just can't stand that crew that's accumulated around him in the last few years. We've got an example on board now of what they do. If you want to know the truth I'm a little scared now that Karlsen's dead."

"Well, we'll soon see them." Holt sighed and stretched. "I'm going to look in on the prisoners. The bridge is yours, Second."

"I relieve you, sir. Do the man a favor and kill him, Thurm."

A minute later, looking through the spy-plate into the courier's small brig, Holt could wish with honest compassion that his male prisoner was dead.

He was an outlaw chieftain named Janda, and his capture had been the last success of Karlsen's Flamland service, putting a virtual end to the rebellion. Janda had been a tall man, a brave rebel, and a brutal bandit. He had raided and fought against Nogara's Esteeler empire until there was no hope left, and then he had surrendered to Karlsen.

"My pride commands me to conquer my enemy," Karlsen had written once, in what he thought was to be a private letter. "My honor forbids me to humble or hate my enemy." But Mical's political police operated with a different philosophy.

The outlaw might still be long-boned, but Holt had never seen him stand tall. The manacles still binding his wrists and ankles were of plastic and supposedly would not abrade human skin, but they served no sane purpose now, and Holt would have removed them if he could.

A stranger seeing the girl Lucinda, who sat now at Janda's side to feed him, might have supposed her to be his daughter. She was his sister, five years younger than he. She was also a girl of rare beauty, and perhaps Mical's police had motives other than mercy in sending her to Nogara's court unmarked and unbrainwashed. It was rumored that the demand for certain kinds of entertainment was strong among the courtiers, and the turnover among the entertainers high.

Holt had so far kept himself from believing such stories, largely by not thinking about them. He opened the brig now—he kept it locked only to prevent Janda's straying out and falling childlike into an accident—and went in.

When the girl Lucinda had first come aboard ship her eyes had shown helpless hatred of every Esteeler. Holt had been as gentle and as helpful as possible to her in the days since then, and there was not even dislike in the face she raised to him now—there was a hope which it seemed she had to share with someone.

She said: "I think he spoke my name a few minutes ago."

"Oh?" Holt bent to look more closely at Janda, and could see no change. The outlaw's eyes still stared glassily, the right eye now and then dripping a tear that seemed to have no connection with any kind of emotion. Janda's jaw was as slack as ever, and his whole body was awkwardly slumped.

"Maybe—" Holt didn't finish.

"What?" She was almost eager.

Gods of Space, he couldn't let himself get involved with this girl. He almost wished to see hatred in her eyes again.

"Maybe," he said gently, "it will be better for your brother if he doesn't make any recovery now. You know where he's going."

Lucinda's hope, such as it was, was shocked away by his words. She was silent, staring at her brother as if she saw something new.

Holt's wrist-intercom sounded.

"Captain here," he acknowledged.

"Sir, reported a ship detected and calling us. Bearing five o'clock level to our course. Small and normal."

The last three words were the customary reassurance that a sighted ship was not possibly a berserker's giant hull. Such Flamland outlaws as were left possessed no deep space ships, so Holt had no reason to be cautious.

He went back to the bridge and looked at the small shape on the detector screen. It was unfamiliar to him, but that was hardly surprising, as there were many shipyards orbiting many planets. Why, though, should any ship approach and hail him in deep space?

Plague?

"No, no plague," answered a radio voice, through bursts of static, when he put the question to the stranger. The video signal from the other ship was also jumpy, making it hard to see the speaker's face. "Caught a speck of dust on my last jump, and my fields are shaky. Will you take a few passengers aboard?"

"Certainly." For a ship on the brink of a C-plus jump to collide with the gravitational field of a sizable dust-speck was a rare accident, but not unheard of. And it would explain the noisy communications. There was still nothing to alarm Holt.

The stranger sent over a launch which clamped to the courier's airlock. Wearing a smile of welcome for distressed passengers, Holt opened the lock. In the next moment he and the half-dozen men who made up his crew were caught helpless by an inrush of metal—a berserker's boarding party, cold and merciless as nightmare.

The machine seized the courier so swiftly and efficiently that no one could offer real resistance, but they did not immediately kill any of the humans. They tore the drive units from one of the lifeboats and herded Holt and his crew and his erstwhile prisoners into the boat.

"It wasn't a berserker on the screen, it wasn't," the

Second Officer kept repeating to Holt. The humans sat side by side, jammed against one another in the small space. The machines were allowing them air and water and food, and had started to take them out one at a time for questioning.

"I know, it didn't look like one," Holt answered. "The berserkers are probably forming themselves into new shapes, building themselves new weapons. That's only logical, after the Stone Place. The only odd thing is that no one foresaw it."

A hatch clanged open, and a pair of roughly man-shaped machines entered the boat, picking their way precisely among the nine cramped humans until they reached the one they wanted.

"No, he can't talk!" Lucinda shrieked. "Don't take him!"

But the machines could not or would not hear. They pulled Janda to his feet and marched him out. The girl followed, dragging at them, trying to argue with them. Holt could only scramble uselessly after her in the narrow space, afraid that one of the machines would turn and kill her. But they only kept her from following them out of the lifeboat, pushing her back from the hatch with metal hands as gently resistless as time. Then they were gone with Janda, and the hatch was closed again. Lucinda stood gazing at it blankly. She did not move when Holt put his arm around her.

After a timeless period of waiting, the humans saw the hatch open again. The machines were back, but they did not return Janda. Instead they had come to take Holt.

Vibrations echoed through the courier's hull; the machines seemed to be rebuilding her. In a small chamber sealed off from the rest of the ship by a new bulkhead, the berserker computer-brain had set up electronic eyes and ears and a speaker for itself, and here Holt was taken to be questioned.

The berserkers interrogated Holt at great length, and almost every question concerned Johann Karlsen. It was known that the berserkers regarded Karlsen as their chief enemy, but this one seemed to be obsessed with him—and unwilling to believe that he was really dead.

"I have captured your charts and astrogational settings," the berserker reminded Holt. "I know your course is to *Nirvana*, where supposedly the nonfunctioning Karlsen has been taken. Describe this *Nirvana*-ship used by the life-unit Nogara."

So long as it had asked only about a dead man, Holt had given the berserker straight answers, not wanting to be tripped up in a useless lie. But a flagship was a different matter, and now he hesitated. Still, there was little he could say about *Nirvana* if he wanted to. And he and his fellow prisoners had had no chance to agree on any plan for deceiving the berserker; certainly it must be listening to everything they said in the lifeboat.

"I've never seen the *Nirvana*," he answered truthfully. "Logic tells me it must be a strong ship, since the highest human leaders travel on it." There was no harm in telling the machine what it could certainly deduce for itself.

A door opened suddenly, and Holt started in surprise as a strange man entered the interrogation chamber. Then he saw that it was not a man, but some creation of the berserker. Perhaps its flesh was plastic, perhaps some product of tissue culture.

"Hi, are you Captain Holt?" asked the figure. There was no gross flaw in it, but a ship camouflaged with the greatest skill looks like nothing so much as a ship that has been camouflaged.

When Holt was silent, the figure asked: "What's wrong?"

Its speech alone would have given it away, to an intelligent human who listened carefully.

"You're not a man," Holt told it.

The figure sat down and went limp.

The berserker explained: "You see I am not capable of making an imitation life-unit that will be accepted by real ones face to face. Therefore I require that you, a real life-unit, help me make certain of Karlsen's death."

Holt said nothing.

"I am a special device," the berserker said, "built by the berserkers with one prime goal, to bring about with certainty Karlsen's death. If you help me prove him dead, I will willingly free you and the other life-units I now hold. If you refuse to help, all of you will receive the most unpleasant stimuli until you change your mind."

Holt did not believe that it would ever willingly set them free. But he had nothing to lose by talking, and he might at least gain for himself and the others a death free of most unpleasant stimuli. Berserkers preferred to be efficient killers, not sadists.

"What sort of help do you want from me?" Holt asked.

"When I have finished building myself into the courier we are going on to *Nirvana*, where you will deliver your prisoners. I have read the orders. After being interviewed by the human leaders on *Nirvana*, the prisoners are to be taken on to Esteel for confinement. Is it not so?"

"It is."

The door opened again, and Janda shuffled in, bent and bemused.

"Can't you spare this man any more questioning?" Holt asked the berserker. "He can't help you in any way."

There was only silence. Holt waited uneasily. At last, looking at Janda, he realized that something about the outlaw had changed. The tears had stopped flowing from his right eye. When Holt saw this he felt a mounting horror that he could not have explained, as if his subconscious already knew what the berserker was going to say next.

"What was bone in this life-unit is now metal," the berserker said. "Where blood flowed, now preservatives are pumped. Inside the skull I have placed a computer, and in the eyes are cameras to gather the evidence I must have on Karlsen. To match the behavior of a brainwashed man is within my capability."

"I do not hate you," Lucinda said to the berserker when it had her alone for interrogation. "You are an accident, like a planet-quake, like a pellet of dust hitting a ship near light-speed. Nogara and his people are the ones I hate. If his brother was not dead I would kill him with my own hands and willingly bring you his body."

"Courier Captain? This is Governor Mical, speaking for the High Lord Nogara. Bring your two prisoners over to *Nirvana* at once."

"At once, sir," Holt acknowledged.

After coming out of C-plus travel within sight of *Nirvana*, the assassin-machine had taken Holt and Lucinda from the lifeboat. Then it had let the boat, with Holt's crew still on it, drift out between the two ships, as if men were using it to check the courier's field. The men on the boat were to be the berserker's hostages, and its shield if it was discovered. And by leaving them there, it doubtless wanted to make more credible the prospect of their eventual release.

Holt had not known how to tell Lucinda of her brother's fate, but at last he had managed somehow. She had wept for a minute, and then she had become very calm.

Now the berserker put Holt and Lucinda into a launch for the trip to *Nirvana*. The machine that had been Lucinda's brother was aboard the launch already, waiting, slumped and broken-looking as the man had been in the last days of his life.

When she saw that figure, Lucinda stopped. Then in a clear voice she said: "Machine, I wish to thank you. You have done my brother a kindness no human would do for him. I think I would have found a way to kill him myself before his enemies could torture him any more."

The *Nirvana*'s airlock was strongly armored, and equipped with automated defenses that would have repelled a rush of boarding machines, just as *Nirvana*'s beams and missiles would have beaten off any heavy-weapons attack a courier, or a dozen couriers, could launch. The berserker had foreseen all this.

An officer welcomed Holt aboard. "This way, Captain. We're all waiting."

"All?"

The officer had the well-fed, comfortable look that came with safe and easy duty. His eyes were busy appraising Lucinda. "There's a celebration under way in the Great Hall. Your prisoners' arrival has been much anticipated."

Music throbbed in the Great Hall, and dancers writhed in costumes more obscene than any nakedness. From a table running almost the length of the Hall, serving machines were clearing the remnants of a feast. In a thronelike chair behind the center of the table sat the High Lord Nogara, a rich cloak thrown over his shoulders, pale wine before him in a crystal goblet. Forty or fifty revelers flanked him at the long table, men and women and a few of whose sex Holt could not at once be sure. All were drinking and laughing, and some were donning masks and costumes, making ready for further celebration.

Heads turned at Holt's entrance, and a moment of silence was followed by a cheer. In all the eyes and faces turned now toward his prisoners, Holt could see nothing like pity.

"Welcome, Captain," said Nogara in a pleasant voice, when Holt had remembered to bow. "Is there news from Flamland?"

"None of great importance, sir."

A puffy-faced man who sat at Nogara's right hand leaned forward on the table. "No doubt there is great mourning for the late governor?"

"Of course, sir." Holt recognized Mical. "And much anticipation of the new."

Mical leaned back in his chair, smiling cynically. "I'm sure the rebellious population is eager for my arrival. Girl, were you eager to meet me? Come, pretty one, round the table, here to me." As Lucinda slowly obeyed, Mical gestured to the serving devices. "Robots, set a chair for the man—there, in the center of the floor. Captain, you may return to your ship."

Felipe Nogara was steadily regarding the manacled figure of his old enemy Janda, and what Nogara might be thinking was hard to say. But he seemed content to let Mical give what orders pleased him.

"Sir," said Holt to Mical. "I would like to see—the remains of Johann Karlsen."

That drew the attention of Nogara, who nodded. A serving machine drew back sable draperies, revealing an alcove in one end of the Hall. In the alcove, before a huge viewport, rested the coffin.

Holt was not particularly surprised; on many planets it was the custom to feast in the presence of the dead. After bowing to Nogara he turned and saluted and walked toward the alcove. Behind him he heard the shuffle and clack of Janda's manacled movement, and held his breath. A muttering passed along the table, and then a sudden quieting in which even the throbbing music ceased. Probably Nogara had gestured permission for Janda's walk, wanting to see what the brainwashed man would do.

Holt reached the coffin and stood over it. He hardly saw the frozen face inside it, or the blur of the hypermass outside the port. He hardly heard the whispers and giggles of the revelers. The only picture clear in his mind showed the faces of his crew as they waited helpless in the grip of the berserker.

The machine clothed in Janda's flesh came shuffling up beside him, and its eyes of glass stared down into those of ice. A photograph of retinal patterns taken back to the waiting berserker for comparison with old captured records would tell it that this man was really Karlsen.

A faint cry of anguish made Holt look back toward the long table, where he saw Lucinda pulling herself away from Mical's clutching arm. Mical and his friends were laughing.

"No, Captain, I am no Karlsen," Mical called down to him, seeing Holt's expression. "And do you think I regret the difference? Johann's prospects are not bright. He is rather bounded by a nutshell, and can no longer count himself king of infinite space!"

"Shakespeare!" cried a sycophant, showing appreciation of Mical's literary erudition.

"Sir." Holt took a step forward. "May I—may I now take the prisoners back to my ship?"

Mical misinterpreted Holt's anxiety. "Oh, ho! I see you appreciate some of life's finer things, Captain. But as you know, rank has its privileges. The girl stays here."

He had expected them to hold on to Lucinda, and she was better here than with the berserker.

"Sir, then if—if the man alone can come with me. In a prison hospital on Esteel he may recover—"

"Captain." Nogara's voice was not loud, but it hushed the table. "Do not *argue* here."

"No, sir."

Mical shook his head. "My thoughts are not yet of mercy to my enemies, Captain. Whether they may soon turn in that direction—well, that depends." He again reached out a leisurely arm to encircle Lucinda. "Do you know, Captain, that hatred is the true spice of love?"

Holt looked helplessly back at Nogara. Nogara's cold eye said: One more word, courier, and you find yourself in the brig. I do not give two warnings.

If Holt cried berserker now, the thing in Janda's shape might kill everyone in the Hall before it could be stopped. He knew it was listening to him, watching his movements.

"I—I am returning to my ship," he stuttered. Nogara looked away, and no one else paid him much attention. "I will . . . return here . . . in a few hours perhaps. Certainly before I drive for Esteel."

Holt's voice trailed off as he saw that a group of the revelers had surrounded Janda. They had removed the manacles from the outlaw's dead limbs, and were putting a horned helmet on his head, giving him a shield and a spear and a cloak of fur, equipage of an old Norse warrior of Earth—first to coin and bear the dread name of berserker.

"Observe, Captain," mocked Mical's voice. "At our masked ball we do not fear the fate of Prince Prospero. We willingly bring in the semblance of the terror outside!"

"Poe!" shouted the sycophant, in glee.

Prospero and Poe meant nothing to Holt, and Mical was disappointed.

"Leave us, Captain," said Nogara, making a direct order of it.

"Leave, Captain Holt," said Lucinda in a firm, clear voice. "We all know you wish to help those who stand in danger here. Lord Nogara, will Captain Holt be blamed in any way for what happens here when he has gone?"

There was a hint of puzzlement in Nogara's clear eyes.

But he shook his head slightly, granting the asked-for absolution.

And there was nothing for Holt to do but go back to the berserker to argue and plead with it for his crew. If it was patient, the evidence it sought might be forthcoming. If only the revelers would have mercy on the thing they thought was Janda.

Holt went out. It had never entered his burdened mind that Karlsen was only frozen.

Mical's arm was about her hips as she stood beside his chair, and his voice purred up at her. "Why, how you tremble, pretty one . . . it moves me that such a pretty one as you should tremble at my touch, yes, it moves me deeply. Now, we are no longer enemies, are we? If we were, I should have to deal harshly with your brother."

She had given Holt time to get clear of the *Nirvana*. Now she swung her arm with all her strength. The blow turned Mical's head halfway round, and made his neat gray hair fly wildly.

There was a sudden hush in the Great Hall, and then a roar of laughter that reddened all of Mical's face to match the handprint on his cheek. A man behind Lucinda grabbed her arms and pinned them. She relaxed until she felt his grip loosen slightly, and then she grabbed up a table knife. There was another burst of laughter as Mical ducked away and the man behind Lucinda seized her again. Another man came to help him and the two of them, laughing, took away the knife and forced her to sit in a chair at Mical's side.

When the governor spoke at last his voice quavered slightly, but it was low and almost calm.

"Bring the man closer," he ordered. "Seat him there, just across the table from us."

While his order was being carried out, Mical spoke to

Lucinda in conversational tones. "It *was* my intent, of course, that your brother should be treated and allowed to recover."

"Lying piece of filth," she whispered, smiling.

Mical only smiled back. "Let us test the skill of my mind-control technicians," he suggested. "I'll wager no bonds will be needed to hold your brother in his chair, once I have done this." He made a curious gesture over the table, toward the glassy eyes that looked out of Janda's face. "So. But he will still be aware, with every nerve, of all that happens to him. You may be sure of that."

She had planned and counted on something like this happening, but now she felt as if she was exhausted from breathing evil air. She was afraid of fainting, and at the same time wished that she could.

"Our guest is bored with his costume." Mical looked up and down the table. "Who will be first to take a turn at entertaining him?"

There was a spattering of applause as a giggling effeminate arose from a nearby chair.

"Jamy is known for his inventiveness," said Mical in pleasant tones to Lucinda. "I insist you watch closely, now. Chin up!"

On the other side of Mical, Felipe Nogara was losing his air of remoteness. As if reluctantly, he was being drawn to watch. In his bearing was a rising expectancy, winning out over disgust.

Jamy came giggling, holding a small jeweled knife.

"Not the eyes," Mical cautioned. "There'll be things I want him to see, later."

"Oh, certainly!" Jamy twittered. He set the horned helmet gingerly aside, and wiped the touch of it from his fingers. "We'll just start like this on one cheek, with a bit of skin—"

Jamy's touch with the blade was gentle, but still too

much for the dead flesh. At the first peeling tug, the whole lifeless mask fell red and wet from around the staring eyes, and the steel berserker-skull grinned out.

Lucinda had just time to see Jamy's body flung across the Hall by a steel-boned arm before the men holding her let go and turned to flee for their lives, and she was able to duck under the table. Screaming bedlam broke loose, and in another moment the whole table went over with a crash before the berserker's strength. The machine, finding itself discovered, thwarted in its primary function of getting away with the evidence on Karlsen, had reverted to the old berserker goal of simple slaughter. It killed efficiently. It moved through the Hall, squatting and hopping grotesquely, mowing its way with scythelike arms, harvesting howling panic into bundles of bloody stillness.

At the main door, fleeing people jammed one another into immobility, and the assassin worked methodically among them, mangling and slaying. Then it turned and came down the Hall again. It came to Lucinda, still kneeling where the table-tipping had exposed her; but the machine hesitated, recognizing her as a semipartner in its prime function. In a moment it had dashed on after another target.

It was Nogara, swaying on his feet, his right arm hanging broken. He had come up with a heavy handgun from somewhere, and now he fired left-handed as the machine charged down the other side of the overturned table toward him. The gunblasts shattered Nogara's friends and furniture but only grazed his moving target.

At last one shot hit home. The machine was wrecked, but its impetus carried it on to knock Nogara down again.

There was a shaky quiet in the Great Hall, which was wrecked as if by a bomb. Lucinda got unsteadily to her feet. The quiet began to give way to sobs and moans and gropings, everywhere, but no one else was standing.

She picked her way dazedly over to the smashed assassin-machine. She felt only a numbness, looking at the rags of clothing and flesh that still clung to its metal frame. Now in her mind she could see her brother's face as it once was, strong and smiling.

Now, there was something that mattered more than the dead, if she could only recall what it was—of course, the berserker's hostages, the good kind spacemen. She could try to trade Karlsen's body for them.

The serving machines, built to face emergencies on the order of spilled wine, were dashing to and fro in the nearest thing to panic that mechanism could achieve. They impeded Lucinda's progress, but she had the heavy coffin wheeled halfway across the Hall when a weak voice stopped her. Nogara had dragged himself up to a sitting position against the overturned table.

He croaked again: "—alive."

"What?"

"Johann's alive. Healthy. See? It's a freezer."

"But we all told the berserker he was dead." She felt stupid with the impact of one shock after another. For the first time she looked down at Karlsen's face, and long seconds passed before she could tear her eyes away. "It has hostages. It wants his body."

"No." Nogara shook his head. "I see, now. But no. I won't give him to berserkers, alive." A brutal power of personality still emanated from his broken body. His gun was gone, but his power kept Lucinda from moving. There was no hatred left in her now.

She protested: "But there are seven men out there."

"Berserkers like me." Nogara bared pain-clenched teeth. "It won't let prisoners go. Here. The key . . ." He pulled it from inside his torn-open tunic.

Lucinda's eyes were drawn once again to the cold serenity of the face in the coffin. Then on impulse she ran to get the key. When she did so Nogara slumped over in relief, unconscious or nearly so.

The coffin lock was marked in several positions, and she turned it to EMERGENCY REVIVAL. Lights sprang on around the figure inside, and there was a hum of power.

By now the automated systems of the ship were reacting to the emergency. The serving machines had begun a stretcher-bearer service, Nogara being one of the first victims they carried away. Presumably a robot medic was in action somewhere. From behind Nogara's throne chair a great voice was shouting:

"This is ship defense control, requesting human orders! What is nature of emergency?"

"Do not contact the courier ship!" Lucinda shouted back. "Watch it for an attack. But don't hit the lifeboat!"

The glass top of the coffin had become opaque.

Lucinda ran to the viewport, stumbling over the body of Mical and going on without a pause. By putting her face against the port and looking out at an angle she could just see the berserker-courier, pinkly visible in the wavering light of the hypermass, its lifeboat of hostages a small pink dot still in place before it.

How long would it wait, before it killed the hostages and fled?

When she turned away from the port, she saw that the coffin's lid was open and the man inside was sitting up. For just a moment, a moment that was to stay in Lucinda's mind, his eyes were like a child's fixed helplessly on hers. Then power began to grow behind his eyes, a power somehow completely different from his brother's and perhaps even greater.

Karlsen looked away from her, taking in the rest of his

surroundings, the devastated Great Hall and the coffin. "Felipe," he whispered, as if in pain, though his half-brother was no longer in sight.

Lucinda moved toward him and started to pour out her story, from the day in the Flamland prison when she had heard that Karlsen had fallen to the plague.

Once he interrupted her. "Help me out of this thing, get me space armor." His arm was hard and strong when she grasped it, but when he stood beside her he was surprisingly short. "Go on, what then?"

She hurried on with her tale, while serving machines came to arm him. "But why were you frozen?" she ended, suddenly wondering at his health and strength.

He ignored the question. "Come along to Defense Control. We must save those men out there."

He went familiarly to the nerve center of the ship and hurled himself into the combat chair of the Defense Officer, who was probably dead. The panel before Karlsen came alight and he ordered at once: "Get me in contact with that courier."

Within a few moments a flat-sounding voice from the courier answered routinely. The face that appeared on the communication screen was badly lighted; someone viewing it without advance warning would not suspect that it was anything but human.

"This is High Commander Karlsen speaking, from the *Nirvana*." He did not call himself governor or lord, but by his title of the great day of the Stone Place. "I'm coming over there. I want to talk to you men on the courier."

The shadowed face moved slightly on the screen. "Yes, sir."

Karlsen broke off the contact at once. "That'll keep its hopes up. Now, I need a launch. You, robots, load my coffin aboard the fastest one available. I'm on emergency revival drugs now and I may have to refreeze for a while."

"You're not really going over there?"

Up out of the chair again, he paused. "I know berserkers. If chasing me is that thing's prime function it won't waste a shot or a second of time on a few hostages while I'm in sight."

"You can't go," Lucinda heard herself saying. "You mean too much to all men—"

"I'm not committing suicide, I have a trick or two in mind." Karlsen's voice changed suddenly. "You say Felipe's not dead?"

"I don't think he is."

Karlsen's eyes closed while his lips moved briefly, silently. Then he looked at Lucinda and grabbed up paper and a stylus from the Defense Officer's console. "Give this to Felipe," he said, writing. "He'll set you and the captain free if I ask it. You're not dangerous to his power. Whereas I . . ."

He finished writing and handed her the paper. "I must go. God be with you."

From the Defense Officer's position, Lucinda watched Karlsen's crystalline launch leave the *Nirvana* and take a long curve that brought it near the courier at a point some distance from the lifeboat.

"You on the courier," Lucinda heard him say. "You can tell it's really me here on the launch, can't you? You can DF my transmission? Can you photograph my retinas through the screen?"

And the launch darted away with a right-angle swerve, dodging and twisting at top acceleration, as the berserker's weapons blasted the space where it had been. Karlsen had been right. The berserker spent not a moment's delay or a single shot on the lifeboat, but hurled itself instantly after Karlsen's launch.

"Hit that courier!" Lucinda screamed. "Destroy it!" A

salvo of missiles left the *Nirvana*, but it was a shot at a receding target, and it missed. Perhaps it missed because the courier was already in the fringes of the distortion surrounding the hypermass.

Karlsen's launch had not been hit, but it could not get away. It was a glassy dot vanishing behind a screen of blasts from the berserker's weapons, a dot being forced into the maelstrom of the hypermass.

"Chase them!" cried Lucinda, and saw the stars tint blue ahead; but almost instantly the *Nirvana*'s autopilot countermanded her order, barking mathematical assurance that to accelerate any further in that direction would be fatal to all aboard.

The launch was now going certainly into the hypermass, gripped by a gravity that could make any engines useless. And the berserker-ship was going headlong after the launch, caring for nothing but to make sure of Karlsen.

The two specks tinted red, and redder still, racing before an enormous falling cloud of dust as if flying into a planet's sunset sky. And then the red shift of the hypermass took them into invisibility, and the universe saw them no more.

Soon after the robots had brought the men from the lifeboat safe aboard *Nirvana*, Holt found Lucinda alone in the Great Hall, gazing out the viewport.

"He gave himself to save you," she said. "And he'd never even seen you."

"I know." After a pause Holt said: "I've just been talking to the Lord Nogara. I don't know why, but you're to be freed, and I'm not to be prosecuted for bringing the damned berserker aboard. Though Nogara seems to hate both of us . . ."

She wasn't listening, she was still looking out the port.

"I want you to tell me all about him someday," Holt

said, putting his arm around Lucinda. She moved slightly, ridding herself of a minor irritation that she had hardly noticed. It was Holt's arm, which dropped away.

"I see," Holt said, after a while. He went to look after his men.

I have seen, and I still see, a future in which you, the Earth-descended, may prevail over the wolves of planets and the wolves of space. For at every stage of your civilizations there are numbers of you who put aside selfishness and dedicate their lives in service to something they see as being greater than themselves.

I say you may prevail, I say not that you will. For in each of your generations there are men who choose to serve the gods of darkness.

IN THE TEMPLE OF MARS

SOMETHING WAS DRIVING WAVES OF CONFUSION THROUGH HIS mind, so that he knew not who he was, or where. How long ago what was happening had started or what had gone before it he could not guess. Nor could he resist what was happening, or even decide if he wanted to resist.

A chant beat on his ears, growled out by barbaric voices:

On the wall there was painted a forest
In which there lived neither man nor beast
With knotty, gnarled, barren trees, old . . .

And he could see the forest around him. Whether the trees and the chanting voices were real or not was a question he could not even formulate, with the confusion patterns racking his mind.

Through broken branches hideous to behold
There ran a cold and sighing sind
As if a storm would break down every bough
And downward, at the bottom of a hill
Stood the temple of Mars who is mighty in arms . . .

And he saw the temple. It was of steel, curved in the dread shape of a berserker's hull, and half-sunken in dark earth. At the entrance, gates of steel sang and shuddered in the cold wind rushing out of the temple, rushing out endlessly to rage through the shattered forest. The whole scene was gray, and lighted from above by an auroral flickering.

The northern lights shone in at the doors
For there was no window on the walls
Through which men might any light discern . . .

He seemed to pass, with a conqueror's strides, between the clawlike gates, toward the temple door.

The door was of eternal adamant
Bound lengthways and sideways with tough iron
And to make the temple stronger, every pillar
Was thick as a barrel, of iron bright and shiny.

The inside of the temple was a kaleidoscope of violence, a frantic abattoir. Hordes of phantasmal men were mowed down in scenes of war, women were slaughtered by machines, children crushed and devoured by animals. He, the conqueror, accepted it all, exulted in it all, even as he became aware that his mind, under some outer compulsion, was building it all from the words of the chant.

He could not tell how long it lasted. The end came abruptly—the pressure on his mind was eased, and the chanting stopped. The relief was such that he fell sprawling, his eyes closed, a soft surface beneath him. Except for his own breathing, all was quiet.

A gentle thud made him open his eyes. A short metal sword had been dropped or tossed from somewhere to land near him. He was in a round, softly lighted, familiar room. The circular wall was covered by a continuous mural, depicting a thousand variations on the theme of bloody violence. At one side of the room, behind a low altar, toward the statue of an armed man gripping chariot reins and battleax, a man who was larger than life and more than a man, his bronze face a mask of insensate rage.

All this he had seen before. He gave it little thought except for the sword. He was drawn to the sword like a steel particle to a magnet, for the power of his recent vision was still fresh and irresistible, and it was the power of destruction. He crawled to the sword, noticing dimly that he was dressed like the statue of the god, in a coat of mail. When he had the sword in his hand the power of it drew him to his feet. He looked round expectantly.

A section of the continuous mural-wall opened into a door, and a figure entered the temple. It was dressed in a neat, plain uniform, and its face was lean and severe. It looked like a man, but it was not a man, for no blood gushed out when the sword hewed in.

Joyfully, thoughtlessly, he hacked the plastic-bodied figure into a dozen pieces. Then he stood swaying over it, drained and weary. The metal pommel of the sword grew suddenly hot in his hand, so that he had to drop it. All this had happened before, again and again.

This painted door opened once more. This time it was a real man who entered, a man dressed in black, who had hypnotic eyes under bushy brows.

"Tell me your name," the black-uniform ordered. His voice compelled.

"My name is Jor."

"And mine?"

"You are Katsulos," said Jor dully, "the Esteeler secret police."

"Yes. And where are we?"

"In space, aboard the *Nirvana II*. We are taking the High Lord Nogara's new space-going castle out to him, out to the rim of the galaxy. And when he comes aboard, I am supposed to entertain him by killing someone with a sword. Or another gladiator will entertain him by killing me."

"Normal bitterness," remarked one of Katsulos' men, appearing in the doorway behind him.

"Yes, this one always snaps right back," Katsulos said. "But a good subject. See the brain rhythms?" He showed the other a torn-off piece of chart from some recording device.

They stood there discussing Jor like a specimen, while he waited and listened. They had taught Jor to behave. They thought they had taught him permanently—but one of these days he was going to show them. Before it was too late. He shivered in his mail coat.

"Take him back to his cell," Katsulos ordered at last. "I'll be along in a moment."

Jor looked about him confusedly as he was led out of the temple and down some stairs. His recollection of the treatment he had just undergone was already becoming uncertain; and what he did remember was so unpleasant that he made no effort to recall more. But his sullen determination to strike back stayed with him, stronger than ever. He had to strike back, somehow, and soon.

Left alone in the temple, Katsulos kicked the pieces of the plastic dummy into a pile, to be ready for careful salvage. He trod heavily on the malleable face, making it unrecognizable, just in case someone beside his own men should happen to see it.

Then he stood for a moment looking up into the maniacal bronze face of Mars. And Katsulos' eyes, that were cold weapons when he turned them on other men, were now alive.

A communicator sounded, in what was to be the High Lord Nogara's cabin when he took delivery of *Nirvana II*. Admiral Hemphill, alone in the cabin, needed a moment to find the proper switch on the huge, unfamiliar desk. "What is it?"

"Sir, our rendezvous with the Solarian courier is completed; we're ready to drive again, unless you have any last-minute messages to transmit?"

"Negative. Our new passenger came aboard?"

"Yes, sir. A Solarian, named Mitchell Spain, as we were advised."

"I know the man, Captain. Will you ask him to come to this cabin as soon as possible? I'd like to talk to him at once."

"Yes sir."

"Are those police still snooping around the bridge?"

"Not at the moment, Admiral."

Hemphill shut off the communicator and leaned back in the thronelike chair from which Felipe Nogara would soon survey his Esteeler empire; but soon the habitually severe expression of Hemphill's lean face deepened and he stood up. The luxury of this cabin did not please him.

On the blouse of Hemphill's neat, plain uniform were seven ribbons of scarlet and black, each representing a battle in which one or more berserker machines had been destroyed. He wore no other decorations except his insignia of rank, granted him by the United Planets, the anti-berserker league, of which all worlds were at least nominal members.

Within a minute the cabin door opened. The man who entered, dressed in civilian clothes, was short and muscular and rather ugly. He smiled at once, and came toward Hemphill, saying: "So it's High Admiral Hemphill now. Congratulations. It's a long time since we've met."

"Thank you. Yes, not since the Stone Place." Hemphill's mouth bent upward slightly at the corners, and he moved around the desk to shake hands. "You were a captain of marines, then, as I recall."

As they gripped hands, both men thought back to that day of victory. Neither of them could smile at it now, for the war was going badly again.

"Yes, that's nine years ago," said Mitchell Spain. "Now—I'm a foreign correspondent for Solar News Service. They're sending me out to interview Nogara."

"I've heard that you've made a reputation as a writer." Hemphill motioned Mitch to a chair. "I'm afraid I have no time myself for literature or other nonessentials."

Mitch sat down, and dug out his pipe. He knew Hemphill well enough to be sure that no slur was intended by the reference to literature. To Hemphill, everything was nonessential except the destruction of berserker machines; and today such a viewpoint was doubtless a good one for a High Admiral.

Mitch got the impression that Hemphill had serious business to talk about, but was uncertain of how to broach the subject. To fill the hesitant silence, Mitch remarked: "I wonder if the High Lord Nogara will be pleased with his new ship." He gestured around the cabin with the stem of his pipe.

Everything was as quiet and steady as if rooted on the surface of a planet. There was nothing to suggest that even now the most powerful engines ever built by Earth-descended man were hurling this ship out toward the rim of the galaxy at many times the speed of light.

Hemphill took the remark as a cue. Leaning slightly forward in his uncomfortable-looking seat, he said: "I'm not concerned about his liking it. What concerns me is how it's going to be used."

Since the Stone Place, Mitch's left hand was mostly scar tissue and prosthetics. He used one plastic finger now to tamp down the glowing coal of his pipe. "You mean Nogara's idea of shipboard fun? I caught a glimpse just now of the gladiatorial arena. I've never met him, but they say he's gone bad, really bad, since Karlsen's death."

"I wasn't talking about Nogara's so-called amusements. What I'm really getting at is this: Johann Karlsen may be still alive."

Hemphill's calm, fantastic statement hung in the quiet cabin air. For a moment Mitch thought that he could sense the motion of the C-plus ship as it traversed spaces no man understood, spaces were it seemed time could mean nothing and the dead of all the ages might still be walking.

Mitch shook his head. "Are we talking about the same Johann Karlsen?"

"Of course."

"Two years ago he went down into a hypermassive sun, with a berserker-controlled ship on his tail. Unless that story's not true?"

"It's perfectly true, except we think now that his launch went into orbit around the hypermass instead of falling into it. Have you seen the girl who's aboard?"

"I passed a girl, outside your cabin here. I thought . . .''

"No, I have no time for that. Her name is Lucinda, single names are the custom on her planet. She's an eye-witness of Karlsen's vanishing."

"Oh. Yes, I remember the story. But what's this about his being in orbit?"

Hemphill stood up and seemed to become more comfortable, as another man would be sitting down. "Ordinarily, the hypermass and everything near it is invisible, due to the extreme red shift caused by its gravity. But during the last year some scientists have done their best to study it. Their ship didn't compare to this one"—Hemphill turned his head for a moment, as if he could hear the mighty engines—"but they went as close as they dared, carrying some new instruments, long-wave telescopes. The star itself was still invisible, but they brought back these."

Hemphill stood behind him. "That's what space looks like near the hypermass. Remember, it has about a billion times the mass of Sol, packed into roughly the same volume. Gravity like that does things we don't yet understand."

"Interesting. What forms these dark lines?"

"Falling dust that's become trapped in lines of gravitic force, like the lines round a magnet. Or so I'm told."

"And where's Karlsen supposed to be?"

Hemphill's finger descended on a photo, pointing out a spot of crystalline roundness, tiny as a raindrop within a magnified line of dust. "We think this is his launch. It's orbiting about a hundred million miles from the center of the hypermass. And the berserker-controlled ship that was chasing him is here, following him in the same dust-line. Now they're both stuck. No ordinary engines can drive a ship down there.''

Mitch stared at the photos, looking past them into old memories that came flooding back. ''And you think he's alive.''

''He had equipment that would let him freeze himself into suspended animation. Also, time may be running quite slowly for him. He's in a three-hour orbit.''

''A three-hour orbit, at a hundred million miles . . . wait a minute.''

Hemphill almost smiled. ''I told you, things we don't understand yet.''

''All right.'' Mitch nodded slowly. ''So you think there's a chance? He's not a man to give up. He'd fight as long as he could, and then invent a way to fight some more.''

''Yes, I think there is a chance.'' Hemphill's face had become iron again. ''You saw what efforts the berserkers made to kill him. They feared him, in their iron guts, as they feared no one else. Though I never quite understood why . . . So, if we can save him, we must do so without delay. Do you agree?''

''Certainly, but how?''

''With this ship. It has the strongest engines ever built— trust Nogara to have seen to that, with his own safety in mind.''

Mitch whistled softly. ''Strong enough to match orbits with Karlsen and pull him out of there?''

''Yes, mathematically. Supposedly.''

''And you mean to make the attempt before this ship is delivered to Nogara.''

''Afterwards may be too late; you know he wanted Karlsen out of the way. With these police aboard I've been keeping my rescue plan a secret.''

Mitch nodded. He felt a rising excitement. "Nogara may rage if we save Karlsen, but they'll be nothing he can do. How about the crew, are they willing?"

"I've already sounded out the captain; he's with me. And since I hold my admiral's rank from the United Planets I can issue legal orders on any ship, if I say I'm acting against berserkers." Hemphill began to pace. "The only thing that worries me is this detachment of Nogara's police we have aboard; they're certain to oppose the rescue."

"How many of them are there?"

"A couple of dozen. I don't know why there are so many, but they outnumber the rest of us two to one. Not counting their prisoners, who of course are helpless."

"Prisoners?"

"About forty young men, I understand. Sword fodder for the arena."

Lucinda spent a good deal of her time wandering, restless and alone, through the corridors of the great ship. Today she happened to be in a passage not far from the central bridge and flag quarters when a door opened close ahead of her and three men came into view. The two who wore black uniforms held a single prisoner, clad in a shirt of chain mail, between them.

When she saw the black uniform, Lucinda's chin lifted. She waited, standing in their path.

"Go round me, vultures," she said in an icy voice when they came up to her. She did not look at the prisoner; bitter experience had taught her that showing sympathy for Nogara's victims could bring added suffering upon them.

The black uniforms halted in front of her. "I am Katsulos," said the bushy-browed one. "Who are you?"

"Once my planet was Flamland," she said, and from the corner of her eye she saw the prisoner's face turn up.

"One day it will be my home again, when it is freed of Nogara's vultures."

The second black uniform opened his mouth to reply, but never got out a word, for just then the prisoner's elbow came smashing back into his belly. Then the prisoner, who till now had stood meek as a lamb, shoved Katsulos off his feet and was out of sight around a bend of corridor before either policeman could recover.

Katsulos bounced quickly to his feet. His gun drawn, he pushed past Lucinda to the bend of the corridor. Then she saw his shoulders slump.

Her delighted laughter did not seem to sting Katsulos in the least.

"There's nowhere he can go," he said. The look in his eyes choked off her laughter in her throat.

Katsulos posted police guards on the bridge and in the engine room, and secured all lifeboats. "The man Jor is desperate and dangerous," he explained to Hemphill and to Mitchell Spain. "Half of my men are searching for him continuously, but you know how big this ship is. I ask you to stay close to your quarters until he's caught."

A day passed, and Jor was not caught. Mitch took advantage of the police dispersal to investigate the arena— Solar News would be much interested.

He climbed a short stair and emerged squinting in imitation sunlight, under a high-domed ceiling as blue as Earth's sky. He found himself behind the upper row of the approximately two hundred seats that encircled the arena behind a sloping crystalline wall. At the bottom of the glassy bowl, the oval-shaped fighting area was about thirty yards long. It was floored by a substance that looked like sand but was doubtless something more cohesive, that would not fly up in a cloud if the artificial gravity chanced to fail.

In this facility as slickly modern as a death-ray the worst

vices of ancient Rome could be most efficiently enjoyed. Every spectator would be able to see every drop of blood. There was only one awkward-looking feature: set at equal intervals around the upper rim of the arena, behind the seats, were three buildings, each as large as a small house. Their architecture seemed to Mitch to belong somewhere on Ancient Earth, not here; their purpose was not immediately apparent.

Mitch took out his pocket camera and made a few photographs from where he stood. Then he walked behind the rows of seats to the nearest of the buildings. A door stood open, and he went in.

At first he thought he had discovered an entrance to Nogara's private harem; but after a moment he saw that the people in the paintings covering the walls were not all, or even most of them, engaged in sexual embraces. There were men and women and godlike beings, posed in a variety of relationships, in the costumes of Ancient Earth when they wore any costumes at all. As Mitch snapped a few more photos he gradually realized that each painted scene was meant to depict some aspect of human love. It was puzzling. He had not expected to find love here, or in any part of Felipe Nogara's chosen environment.

As he left the temple through another door, he passed a smiling statue, evidently the resident goddess. She was bronze, and the upper part of her beautiful body emerged nude from glittering sea-green waves. He photographed her and moved on.

The second building's interior paintings showed scenes of hunting and of women in childbirth. The goddess of this temple was clothed modestly in bright green, and armed with a bow and quiver. Bronze hounds waited at her feet, eager for the chase.

As he moved on to the last temple, Mitch found his

steps quickening slightly. He had the feeling that something was drawing him on.

Whatever attraction might have existed was annihilated
in revulsion as soon as he stepped into the place. If the
first building was a temple raised to love, surely this one
honored hate.

On the painted wall opposite the entrance, a sowlike
beast thrust its ugly head into a cradle, devouring the
screaming child. Beside it, men in togas, faces glowing
with hate, stabbed one of their number to death. All
around the walls men and women and children suffered
pointlessly and died horribly, without hope. The spirit of
destruction was almost palpable within this room. It was
like a berserker's—

Mitch took a step back and closed his eyes, bracing his
arms against the sides of the entrance. Yes, he could feel
it. Something more than painting and lighting had been set
to work here, to honor Hate. Something physical, that
Mitch found not entirely unfamiliar.

Years ago, during a space battle, he had experienced the
attack of a berserker's mind beam. Men had learned how
to shield their ships from mind beams—did they now bring
the enemy's weapons inside deliberately?

Mitch opened his eyes. The radiation he felt now was
very weak, but it carried something worse than mere
confusion.

He stepped back and forth through the entrance. Outside
the thick walls of the temple, thicker than those of the
other buildings, the effect practically disappeared. Inside,
it was definitely perceptible, an energy that pricked at the
rage centers of the brain. Slowly, slowly, it seemed to be
fading, like a residual charge from a machine that had
been turned off. If he could feel it now, what must this
temple be like when the projector was on?

More importantly, why was such a thing here at all?

Only to goad a few gladiators on to livelier deaths? Possibly. Mitch glanced at this temple's towering bronze god, riding his chariot over the world, and shivered. He suspected something worse than the simple brutality of Roman games.

He took a few more pictures, and then remembered seeing an intercom station near the first temple he had entered. He walked back there, and punched out the number of Ship's Records on the intercom keys.

When the automated voice answered, he ordered: "I want some information about the design of this arena, particularly the three structures spaced around the upper rim."

The voice asked if he wanted diagrams.

"No. At least not yet. Just tell me what you can about the designer's basic plan."

There was a delay of several seconds. Then the voice said: "The basic designer was a man named Oliver Mical, since deceased. In his design programming, frequent reference is made to descriptive passages within a literary work by one Geoffrey Chaucer of Ancient Earth. The quote fantastic unquote work is titled The Knight's Tale."

The name of Chaucer rang only the faintest of bells for Mitch. But he remembered that Oliver Mical had been one of Nogara's brainwashing experts, and also a classical scholar.

"What kind of psychoelectronic devices are built into these three structures?"

"There is no record aboard of any such installation."

Mitch was sure about the hate-projector. It might have been built in secretly; it probably *had* been, if his worst suspicions were true.

He ordered: "Read me some of the relevant passages of this literary work."

"The three temples are those of Mars, Diana, and

Venus," said the intercom. "A passage relevant to the temple of Mars follows, in original language:

"First on the wal was peynted a forest
In which there dwelleth neither man ne beast
With knotty, knarry, barreyn trees olde
Of stubbes sharp and hidous to biholde."

Mitch knew just enough of ancient languages to catch a word here and there, but he was not really listening now. His mind had stopped on the phrase "temple of Mars." He had heard it before, recently, applied to a newly risen secret cult of berserker-worshippers.

"And downward from a hill, under a bente
Ther stood the temple of Mars armipotente
Wrought all of burned steel, of which the entree
Was long and streit, and gastly for to see."

There was a soft sound behind Mitch, and he turned quickly. Katsulos stood there. He was smiling, but his eyes reminded Mitch of Mars' statue.

"Do you understand the ancient language, Spain? No? Then I shall translate." He took up the verse in a chanting voice:

"Then saw I first the dark imagining
Of felony, and all its compassing
The cruel ire, red as any fire
The pickpurse, and also the pale dread
The smiler with the knife under his cloak
The stable burning with the black smoke
The treason of the murdering in the bed
The open war, with all the wounds that bled . . ."

"Who are you, really?" Mitch demanded. He wanted it out in the open. And he wanted to gain time, for Katsulos wore a pistol at his belt. "What is this to you? Some kind of religion?"

"Not *some* religion!" Katsulos shook his head, while his eyes glowed steadily at Mitch. "Not a mythology of distant gods, not a system of pale ethics for dusty philosophers. No!'' He took a step closer. "Spain, there is no time now for me to proselyte with craft and subtlety. I say only this—the temple of Mars stands open to you. The new god of all creation will accept your sacrifice and your love.''

"You pray to that bronze statue?'' Mitch shifted his weight slightly, getting ready.

"No!'' The fanatic's words poured out faster and louder. "The figure with helmet and sword is our symbol and no more. Our god is new, and real, and worthy. He wields deathbeam and missile, and his glory is as the nova sun. He is the descendant of Life, and feeds on Life as is his right. And we who give ourselves to any of his units become immortal in him, though our flesh perish at his touch!''

"I've heard there were men who prayed to berserkers,'' said Mitch. "Somehow I never expected to meet one.'' Faintly in the distance he heard a man shouting, and feet pounding down a corridor. Suddenly he wondered if he, or Katsulos, was more likely to receive reinforcement.

"Soon we will be everywhere,'' said Katsulos loudly. "We are here now, and we are seizing this ship. We will use it to save the unit of our god orbiting the hypermass. And we will give the badlife Karlsen to Mars, and we will give ourselves. And through Mars we will live forever!''

He looked into Mitch's face and started to draw his gun, just as Mitch hurled himself forward.

Katsulos tried to spin away, Mitch failed to get a solid grip on him, and both men fell sprawling. Mitch saw the gun muzzle swing round on him, and dived desperately for shelter behind a row of seats. Splinters flew around him as the gun blasted. In an instant he was moving again, in a crouching run that carried him into the temple of Venus by one door and out by another. Before Katsulos could sight at him for another shot, Mitch had leaped down an exit stairway, out of the arena.

As he emerged into a corridor, he heard gunfire from the direction of the crew's quarters. He went the other way, heading for Hemphill's cabin. At a turn in the passage a black uniform stepped out to bar his way, aiming a pistol. Mitch charged without hesitation, taking the policeman by surprise. The gun fired as Mitch knocked it aside, and then his rush bowled the black-uniform over. Mitch sat on the man and clobbered him with fists and elbows until he was quiet.

Then, captured gun in hand, Mitch hurried on to Hemphill's door. It slid open before he could pound on it, and closed again as soon as he had jumped inside.

A dead black-uniform sat leaning against the wall, unseeing eyes aimed at Mitch, bullet-holes patterned across his chest.

"Welcome," said Hemphill drily. He stood with his left hand on an elaborate control console that had been raised from a place of concealment inside the huge desk. In his right hand a machine pistol hung casually. "It seems we face greater difficulties than we expected."

Lucinda sat in the darkened cabin that was Jor's hiding place, watching him eat. Immediately after his escape she had started roaming the ship's passages, looking for him, whispering his name, until at last he had answered her. Since then she had been smuggling him food and drink.

He was older than she had thought at first glance; a man of about her own age, with tiny lines at the corners of his suspicious eyes. Paradoxically, the more she helped him, the more suspicious his eyes became.

Now he paused in his eating to ask: "What do you plan to do when we reach Nogara, and a hundred men come aboard to search for me? They'll soon find me, then."

She wanted to tell Jor about Hemphill's plan for rescuing Karlsen. Once Johann Karlsen was aboard, no one on this ship would have to fear Nogara, or so she felt. But just because Jor still seemed suspicious of her, she hesitated to trust him with a secret.

"You knew you'd be caught eventually," she countered. "So why did you run away?"

"You don't know what it's like, being their prisoner."

"I do know."

He ignored her contradiction. "They trained me to fight in the arena with the others. And then they singled me out, and began to train me for something even worse. Now they flick a switch somewhere, and I start to kill, like a berserker."

"What do you mean?"

He closed his eyes, his food forgotten. "I think there's a man they want me to assassinate. Every day or so they put me in the temple of Mars and drive me mad, and then the image of this man is always sent to me. Always it's the same face and uniform. And I must destroy the image, with a sword or a gun or with my hands. I have no choice when they flip that switch, no control over myself. They've hollowed me out and filled me up with their own madness. They're madmen. I think they go into the temple themselves, and turn the foul madness on, and wallow in it, before their idol."

He had never said so much to her in one speech before. She was not sure how much of it was true, but she felt he believed it all. She reached for his hand.

"Jor, I do know something about them. That's why I've helped you. And I've seen other men who were really brainwashed. They haven't really destroyed you, you'll be all right again someday."

"They want me to look normal." He opened his eyes,

which were still suspicious. "Why are you on this ship, anyway?"

"Because." She looked into the past. "Two years ago I met a man called Johann Karlsen. Yes, the one everyone knows of. I spent about ten minutes with him . . . if he's still alive, he's certainly forgotten me, but I fell in love with him."

"In love!" Jor snorted, and began to pick his teeth.

Or I thought I fell in love, she said to herself. Watching Jor now, understanding and forgiving his sullen mistrust, she realized she was no longer able to visualize Karlsen's face clearly.

Something triggered Jor's taut nerves, and he jumped up to peek out of the cabin into the passage. "What's that noise? Hear? It sounds like fighting."

"So." Hemphill's voice was grimmer than usual. "The surviving crewmen are barricaded in their quarters, surrounded and under attack. The damned berserker-lovers hold the bridge, and the engine room. In fact they hold the ship, except for this." He patted the console that he had raised from concealment inside Nogara's innocent-looking desk. "I know Felipe Nogara, and I thought he'd have a master control in his cabin, and when I saw all the police I thought I might possibly need it. That's why I quartered myself in here."

"What all does it control?" Mitch asked, wiping his hands. He had just dragged the dead man into a closet. Katsulos should have known better than to send only one against the High Admiral.

"I believe it will override any control on the bridge or in the engine room. With it I can open or close most of the doors and hatches on the ship. And there seem to be scanners hidden in a hundred places, connected to this little viewscreen. The berserker-lovers aren't going anywhere with this ship until they've done a lot of rewiring or gotten us out of this cabin.''

"I don't suppose we're going anywhere either," said Mitch. "Have you any idea what's happened to Lucy?"

"No. She and that man Jor may be free, and they may do us some good, but we can't count on it. Spain, look here." Hemphill pointed to the little screen. "This is a view inside the guardroom and prison, under the arena's seats. If all those individual cells are occupied, there must be about forty men in there.''

"That's an idea. They may be trained fighters, and they'll certainly have no love for the black uniforms.''

"I could talk to them from here," Hemphill mused. "But how can we free them and arm them? I can't control their individual cell doors, though I can keep the enemy locked out of that area, at least for a while. Tell me, how did the fighting start? What set it off?''

Mitch told Hemphill what he knew. "It's almost funny. The cultists have the same idea you have, of taking this ship out to the hypermass and going after Karlsen. Only of course they want to give him to the berserkers." He shook his head. "I suppose Katsulos hand-picked cultists from among the police for this mission. There must be more of them around than any of us thought.''

Hemphill only shrugged. Maybe he understood fairly well those fanatics out there whose polarity happened to be opposite from his own.

Lucinda would not leave Jor now, nor let him leave her. Like hunted animals they made their way through the corridors, which she knew well from her days of restless walking. She guided him around the sounds of fighting to where he wanted to go.

He peered around the last corner, and brought his head back to whisper: "There's no one at the guardroom door.''

"But how will you get in? And some of the vultures may be inside, and you're not armed."

He laughed soundlessly. "What have I to lose? My *life?*" He moved on around the corner.

Mitch's fingers suddenly dug into Hemphill's arm. "Look! Jor's there, with the same idea you had. Open the door for him, quick!"

Most of the painted panels had been removed from the interior walls of the temple of Mars. Two black-uniformed men were at work upon the mechanism thus revealed, while Katsulos sat at the altar, watching Jor's progress through his own secret scanners. When he saw Jor and Lucinda being let into the guardroom, Katsulos pounced.

"Quick, turn on the beam and focus on him. Boil his brain with it! He'll kill everyone in there, and then we can take our time with the others."

Katsulos' two assistants hurried to obey, arranging cables and a directional antenna. One asked: "He's the one you were training to assassinate Hemphill?"

"Yes. His brain rhythms are on the chart. Focus on him quickly!"

"Set them free and arm them!" Hemphill's image shouted, from a guardroom viewscreen. "You men there! Fight with us and I promise to take you to freedom when the ship is ours; and I promise we'll take Johann Karlsen with us, if he's alive."

There was a roar from the cells at the offer of freedom, and another roar at Karlsen's name. "With him, we'd go on to Esteel itself!" one prisoner shouted.

When the beam from the temple of Mars struck downward, it went unfelt by everyone but Jor. The others in the guardroom had not been conditioned by repeated treatments, and the heat of their emotions was already high.

Just as Jor picked up the keys that would open the cells, the beam hit him. He knew what was happening, but there was nothing he could do about it. In a paroxysm of rage he dropped the keys, and grabbed an automatic weapon from the arms rack. He fired at once, shattering Hemphill's image from the viewscreen.

With the fragment of his mind that was still his own, Jor felt despair like that of a drowning man. He knew he was not going to be able to resist what was coming next.

When Jor fired at the viewscreen, Lucinda understood what was being done to him.

"Jor, no!" She fell to her knees before him. The face of Mars looked down at her, frightening beyond anything she had ever seen. But she cried out to Mars: "Jor, stop! I love you!"

Mars laughed at her love, or tried to laugh. But Mars could not quite manage to point the weapon at her. Jor was trying to come back into his own face again, now coming back halfway, struggling terribly.

"And you love me, Jor. I know. Even if they force you to kill me, remember I know that."

Jor, clinging to his fragment of sanity, felt a healing power come to him, setting itself against the power of Mars. In his mind danced the pictures he had once glimpsed inside the temple of Venus. Of course! There must be a countering projector in there, and someone had managed to turn it on.

He made the finest effort he could imagine. And then, with Lucinda before him, he made a finer effort still.

He came above his red rage like a swimmer surfacing, lungs bursting, from a drowning sea. He looked down at his hands, at the gun they held. He forced his fingers to begin opening. Mars still shouted at him, louder and louder, but Venus' power grew stronger still. His hands opened and the weapon fell.

Once the gladiators had been freed and armed the fight was soon over, though not one of the cultists even tried to surrender. Katsulos and the two with him him fought to the last from inside the temple of Mars, with the hate projector at maximum power, and the recorded chanting voices roaring out their song. Perhaps Katsulos still hoped to drive his enemies to acts of self-destructive rage, or perhaps he had the projector on as an act of worship.

Whatever his reasons, the three inside the temple absorbed the full effect themselves. Mitch had seen bad things before, but when he at last broke open the temple door, he had to turn away for a moment.

Hemphill showed only satisfaction at seeing how the worship of Mars had culminated aboard *Nirvana II*. "Let's see to the bridge and the engine room first. Then we can get this mess cleaned up and be on our way."

Mitch was glad to follow, but he was detained for a moment by Jor.

"Was it you who managed to turn on the counter-projector? If it was, I owe you much more than my life."

Mitch looked at him blankly. "Counter-projector? What're you talking about?"

"But there must have been . . ."

When the others had hurried away, Jor remained in the arena, looking in awe at the thin walls of the temple of Venus, where no projector could be hidden. Then a girl's voice called, and Jor too hurried out.

There was a half minute of silence in the arena.

"Emergency condition concluded," said the voice of the intercom station, to the rows of empty seats. "Ship's records returning to normal operation. Last question asked

concerned basis of temple designs. Chaucer's verse relevant to temple of Venus follows, in original language:

"I recche nat if it may bettre be
To have victorie of them, or they of me
So that I have myne lady in myne armes.
For though so be that Mars is god of Armes,
Your vertu is so great in hevene above
That, if yow list, I shall wel have my love . . ."

Venus smiled, half-risen from her glittering waves.

BROTHER BERSERKER

THE BAREFOOT MAN IN THE GRAY FRIAR'S HABIT REACHED THE top of a rise and paused, taking a look at the country ahead of him. In that direction, the paved road he was following continued to run almost straight under a leaden sky, humping over one gentle hill after another, cutting through scrubby woods and untended fields. The stones of this road had been laid down in the days of glory of the great Continental Empire; there was not much else in the world that had survived the centuries between then and now.

From where the friar stood, the road appeared to be aimed at a slender tower, a sharp and lonely temple spire, gray and vague in the day's dull light, which rose from an unseen base at some miles' distance. The friar had walked with that spire in sight for half a day already, but his goal still lay far beyond.

The friar was of medium height and wiry build. His appearance seemed to have little relation to his age; he might have been anywhere between twenty and forty. His scantily bearded face was tired now, and his gray robe was spotted with mud of darker gray. Here along the shoulders of the road the fields were all ankle-deep in mud, and they showed no sign of having been plowed or planted this spring or last.

"Oh, Holy One, I thank you again that I have had this pavement to follow for so much of my journey," the friar murmured, as he started forward again. The soles of his feet looked as scarred and tough as those of well-used hiking boots.

Except for the distant spire, the only sign of any recent

human presence in this unpromising landscape was a heap of low, ruined walls at roadside just ahead. Only the fact of ruin was recent; the walls themselves were old and might have been a part of a caravanserai or military post in the days of the Empire's strength. But last month or last tenday a new war had passed this way, dissolving one more building into raw tumbled stones. What was left of the structure looked as if it might be going to sink without a trace into the mud, even before the spring grass could start to grow around the foundations.

The friar sat down on the remnant of the old wall, resting from his journey and looking with minor sadness at the minor destruction about him. After a bit, in the manner of one who cannot sit entirely still for very long, he leaned over and took one of the fallen stones in his lean strong hands. Looking at the stone with what might have been a mason's practiced eye, he fitted it deftly into a notch in the stump of wall and sat back to study the effect.

A distant hail made him raise his head and look back along the way he had come. Another lone figure, dressed in a habit much like his own, was hastening toward him, waving both arms for attention.

The first friar's thin face lighted gently at the prospect of company. He returned the wave and waited, forgetting his little game of masonry. Soon he got to his feet.

Presently the approaching figure resolved itself into a man of middle height, who was almost stout and who had recently been clean-shaven. "Glory to the Holy One, revered Brother!" puffed this newcomer, as he arrived at last within easy talking distance.

"Glory to His name." The bearded friar's voice was warm but unremarkable.

The portly one, a man of about thirty, seated himself heavily on the low wall, wiped at his face, and inquired anxiously, "Are you, as I think, Brother Jovann of Ernard?"

"That is my name."

"Now may the Holy One be praised!" The heavier man made a wedge-sign with his hands and rolled his eyes heavenward. "My name is Saile, brother. Now may the Holy One be praised, say I—"

"So be it."

"—for He has led me in mysterious ways to reach your side! And many more shall follow. Brother Jovann, men will flock to you from the four corners of the world, for the fame of your heroic virtue has spread far, to the land of Mosnar, or so I have heard, and even to the lands of the infidel. And here in our own land—even at this moment, in the isolated villages of these remote hills—some of the most backward peasants are aware of your passage."

"I fear my many faults are also known hereabouts, for I was born not far away."

"Ah, Brother Jovann, you are overly modest. During my arduous struggles to reach your side, I have heard again and again of your holy exploits."

Brother Jovann, his face showing some concern, sat down on the wall again. "Why have you struggled, as you say, to reach my side?"

"Ahh." What a struggle it had been, said Saile's headshake. "The flame of my determination was first kindled several months ago, when I was told by unimpeachable sources, eyewitnesses, how, when you were with the army of the Faithful in the field, you dared to leave the sheltering ranks, to cross no-man's-land into the very jaws of the infidel; there to enter the tent of the arch-infidel himself and preach to him the truth of our Holy Temple!"

"And to fail to convert him." Jovann nodded sadly. "You do well to remind me of my failure, for I am prone to the sin of pride."

"Ah." Saile lost headway, but only for a moment. "It

was, as I say, upon hearing of that exploit, Brother Jovann, that it became my own most humble wish, my most burning and holy ambition, to seek you out, to be among the very first to join your order.'' Saile's eyebrows went up questioningly. ''Ah, it is true, then, that you *are* on your way to Empire City even now, to petition our most holy Vicar Nabur for permission to found a new religious order?''

The thin friar's eyes looked toward the spire in the distance. ''Once, Brother, God called me to rebuild fallen temples with stone and brick. Now, as you say, I am called to rebuild with men.'' His attention came back to Brother Saile, and he was smiling. ''As for your becoming a member of the new order when it is formed, why, I can say nothing yet of that. But if you should choose to walk with me to Empire City, I will be happy for your company.''

Saile jumped to his feet, to bob up and down with bowing. ''It is I who am most happy and most honored, Brother Jovann!''

Saile prolonged his thanks as the two men walked on together. He had then commented at some length on the unpleasant prospect of yet more rain falling and was discoursing on the problem of where, in this deserted-looking land, two mendicant friars might hope to obtain their next meal, when there occurred a distraction.

A speedy coach was overtaking them on the road. The vehicle was not ornate, but it was well built, looking as if it might belong to some nobleman or prelate of lower-middle rank. The friars' ears gave them plenty of warning to step aside; four agile load-beasts were making the wheels clatter over the leveled stones at a good speed.

As the coach rumbled past, Brother Jovann felt his eyes drawn to the face of an occupant who rode facing forward, with his head visible in profile and one elbow extended slightly from a window. So far as could be judged, this man was of stocky build. He was well dressed, old and

gray-bearded, though the short-cut hair on his head was
still of ginger color. His thick mouth was twisted slightly,
as if ready to spit or to dispute.

"They might have given us a lift," Brother Saile muttered unhappily, looking after the coach as it dwindled into
the distance. "Plenty of room. There were no more than
two passengers, were there?"

Brother Jovann shook his head, not having noticed
whether there had been any other passengers. His attention
had been held by the old man's eyes, which had probably
never seen the friars at all. Those eyes, fixed in the
direction of the Holy City a hundred miles and more away,
were clear and gray and powerful. But they were also very
much afraid.

When Derron Odegard walked out on the victory celebration at Time Operations, he had no clear idea of where
he was going. Only when he found himself approaching
the nearby hospital complex did he realize that his feet
were taking him to Lisa. Yet, it would be best to face her
at once and get it over with.

At the student nurses' quarters he learned that she had
moved out the day before, after having gotten permission
to drop out of training there. While being tested and
considered for other jobs, she was sharing a cubicle with
another girl in a low-rank, uplevel corridor.

It was Lisa's new roommate who opened the door to
Derron's knock; since the girl was in the midst of doing
something to her hair, she went back inside the cubicle and
pretended not to be listening.

Lisa must have seen Derron's news in his face. Her own
face at once became as calm as a mask, and she remained
just inside the half-open door, letting him stand in the
narrow corridor to be brushed by the curious and incurious
passers-by.

"It's Matt," he said to her. When there was no reaction, he went on. "Oh, the battle's won. The berserkers are stopped. But he sacrificed himself to do it. He's dead."

Proud and hard as a shield, her mask-face lifted slightly toward him. "Of course he is. He did the job you gave him. I knew he would."

"Understand, Lisa—when I went to him with that sales talk I thought he was going to have a chance, a good chance."

She was not going to be able to keep the shield up, after all; with something like relief he saw her face begin to move and heard her voice begin to break. She said, "I—knew you were going to kill him."

"My God, Lisa, that wasn't what I meant to do!" He kept his hands from reaching out to her.

Slowly dissolving and melting into a woman's grief, she leaned against the doorjamb, her hands hidden behind her. "And now—there's—n-nothing to be done!"

"The doctors tried—but no, nothing. And Operations can't go back to do anything for Matt in the past—it'd wreck the world if we tried to pull him out of that mess now."

"The world's not worth it!"

He was murmuring some banality, and had reached out at last to try to comfort her, when the door slammed in his face.

If Lisa was the woman he needed, he would have stayed there; so he thought to himself a few days later as he sat alone in his tiny private office on the Operations Level. He would have stayed and made her open the door again or else kicked it down. It was only a door of plastic, and behind it she was still alive.

The fact was, of course, that the woman he did need had

been for a year and more behind the door of death. And no man could smash through that. A man could only stand before that door and mourn, until he found that he was able to turn away.

Derron had been sitting in his office staring into space for some little time before he noticed an official-looking envelope that some courier must have left on his small desk. The envelope was neat and thick, sealed and addressed to him. After looking inertly at it for a while he took it up and opened it.

Inside was the formal notice of his latest promotion, to the rank of lieutenant colonel. ". . . in consideration of your recent outstanding service in Time Operations, and in the expectation that you will continue . . ." A set of appropriate collar insignia was enclosed.

The insignia held in his hand as if forgotten, he sat there a while longer, looking across the room at an object—it was an ancient battle-helmet, ornamented with wings—that rested like a trophy atop his small bookcase. He was still doing this when the clangor of the alert signal sounded throughout Operations and pulled him reflexively to his feet. In another moment he was out the door and on his way to the briefing room.

Latecomers were still hurrying in when a general officer, Time Ops' chief of staff, mounted the dais and began to speak.

"The third assault we've been expecting has begun, gentlemen. Win or lose, this will be the last attack the berserkers can mount outside of present-time. It'll give us the final bearing we need to locate their staging area twenty-one thousand years down."

There were a few scattered expressions of optimism.

"I suggest that you don't cheer yet. This third attack gives every indication of involving some new tactics on the enemy's part, something subtle and extremely dangerous.''

The general performed the usual unveiling of some hastily assembled maps and models. "Like the previous attack, this one is aimed at a single individual; and, again, there's no doubt about the target's identity. This time the name is Vincent Vincento.''

There was a murmur at that name, a ripple of awe and wonder and concern. There would have been a similar reaction from almost any audience that might have been assembled on Sirgol. Even the half-educated of that world had heard of Vincento, though the man was some three hundred years dead and had never ruled a nation, started a religion, or raised an army.

Derron's attention became sharply focused, and he sat up straighter, his feeling of inertia slipping away. In his prewar historical studies he had specialized in Vincento's time and place—and that locale was also oddly connected with his private grief.

The general on the dais spoke on, in businesslike tones. "Vincento's lifeline is among the very few ultraimportant ones for which we have provided continuous sentry protection along their entire effective lengths. Of course, this doesn't mean that a berserker can't get near him. But should one of them try to do violent harm to Vincento, or even to any other person within a couple of miles of him, we'd be on to its keyhole in a couple of seconds and cancel it out. The same thing applies if they should try to kidnap or capture Vincento himself.

"This special protection actually starts back in Vincento's grandparents' time and runs along his lifeline until his completion of his last important work at the age of seventy-eight, and we can assume the enemy knows that this protection exists. That's why I said that this time the berserkers' plans are no doubt subtle.''

After going into the technical details of the sentry protection against direct violence, the general moved on to discuss another point. "Chronologically, the enemy penetration is not more than a tenday before the start of Vincento's famous trial by the Defenders of the Faith. This may well be more than a coincidence. Suppose, for example, that a berserker could alter the outcome of this trial to a death sentence for Vincento. If the Defenders should decide to burn him at the stake, the berserker's part in his death would be too indirect to give us any help in finding its keyhole.

"And also remember—an actual death sentence would not seem to be necessary for the enemy's purpose. Vincento at the time of his trial is seventy years old. If he should be put to torture or thrown into a dungeon, the odds are high that his life would be effectively ended."

A general seated in the front row raised his hand. "Doesn't he historically undergo some such treatment?"

"No. That's a fairly common idea. But, historically, Vincento never spent a day of his life in prison. During his trial he occupied a friendly ambassador's quarters. And after his recantation, he passed the few years left to him in physically comfortable house arrest. There he gradually went blind, from natural causes—and also laid the foundation of the science of dynamics. On that work of his, needless to say, our modern science and our survival most heavily depend. Make no mistake about it, those last years of Vincento's life after his trial are vital to us."

The questioning general shifted in his front rank chair. "How in the world is an alien machine going to influence the outcome of a trial in an ecclesiastical court?"

The briefing officer could only shake his head and stare gloomily at his charts. "Frankly, we've still a shortage of good ideas on that. We doubt that the enemy will try again to play a supernatural role, after the failure of their last attempt along that line.

"But here's an angle worth keeping in mind. Only one enemy device is engaged in this attack, and from all screen indications it's a physically small machine, only about the size of a man. Which immediately suggests to us the possibility that this one may be an android." The speaker paused to look round at his audience. "Oh, yes, I know, the berserkers have never, anywhere, been able to fabricate an android that would pass in human society as a normal person. Still, we hardly dare rule out the possibility that this time they've succeeded."

A discussion got going on possible countermeasures. A whole arsenal of devices were being kept in readiness in Stage Two for dropping into the past, but no one could say yet what might be needed.

The briefing officer pushed his charts aside for the moment. "The one really bright spot, of course, is that this attack lies within the time band where we can drop live agents. So naturally we'll count on putting men on the spot as our main defense. Their job will be to keep their eyes on Vincento from a little distance; they'll be people able to spot any significant deviation from history when they see it. Those we choose as agents will need to know that particular period very well, besides having experience in Time Operations. . . ."

Listening, Derron looked down at the new insignia he was still carrying in his hand. And then he began at last to fasten them on.

About two miles along the road from the spot where they had met, Brother Jovann and Brother Saile topped yet another rise and discovered that they were about to catch up with the coach that had passed them so speedily not long before. Its load-beasts unharnessed and grazing nearby, the vehicle stood empty beside the broken gate of a high-walled enclosure, which crouched under slate roofs at the foot of the next hill ahead.

Atop that hill there rose the already famed cathedral-temple of Oibbog, much of its stonework still too new to bear moss or signs of weathering. Holding its spire now immense and overshadowing against the lowering sky, the graceful mass seemed almost to float, secure above all human effort and concern.

The ancient road, after passing the broken gate of the monastery at the foot of the new cathedral's hill, swerved left to meet a bridge. Or the stub of a bridge, rather. From where the friars now stood they could see that all of the spans were gone, together with four of the six piers that had supported them. The river that had torn them down was raging still, jamming tree trunks like forked spears against the supports that remained. Obviously swollen to several times its normal flow, the current was ravaging the lowlands on both its banks.

On the other side of the torrent, beyond another stub of bridge, the walled town of Oibbog sat secure on its high ground. People could be seen moving here and there in those distant streets. Inside the town's gate, which opened on the Empire road, more coaches and load-beasts waited, having been interrupted in journeys outbound from the Holy City.

Brother Jovann watched leaden clouds still mounting ominously up the sky. Fleeing from these clouds was the river, a great swollen terrified snake being lashed and goaded by distant flails of lightning, a snake that had burst its bonds and carried them away.

"Brother River will not let us cross tonight."

When he heard this personification, Brother Saile turned his head slowly and cautiously around, as if he wondered whether he was expected to laugh. But before he had time to decide, the rain broke again, like a waterfall. Tucking up the skirts of their robes, both friars ran. Jovann sprinted barefoot, Saile with sandals flapping, to join the occupants of the coach in whatever shelter the abandoned-looking monastery might afford.

A hundred miles away, in what had been the capital of the vanished Empire and was now the Holy City of the embattled Temple, the same day was warm and sultry. Only the wrath of Nabur the Eighth, eighty-first in the succession of Vicars of the Holy One, stirred like a storm wind the air of his luxurious private apartments.

This wrath had been some time accumulating, thought Defender Belam, who stood in robes of princely scarlet, waiting in silent gravity for it to be over. It had been accumulated and saved up till now, when it could be discharged harmlessly, vented into the discreet ears of a most trusted auditor and friend.

The vicar's peripatetic tirade against his military and theological opponents broke off in mid-sentence; Nabur was distracted, and his pacing stopped, by a dull scraping sound, ending in a heavy thud, which floated in from outside, accompanied by the shouts of workmen. The vicar moved to look down from a balconied window into a courtyard. Earlier, Belam had seen the workmen down there, starting to unload some massive blocks of marble from a train of carts. Today a famed sculptor was to choose one block, and then begin work on Nabur's portrait-statue.

What did it matter if each of eighty predecessors had been willing to let their worldly glorification wait upon posterity?

The vicar turned from the balcony suddenly, the skirts of his simple white robe swirling, and caught Belam wearing a disapproving face.

In his angry tenor, which for the past forty years had sounded like an old man's voice, the vicar declaimed, "When the statue is completed we will have it placed in the city's Great Square, that the majesty of our office and our person may be increased in the eyes of the people!"

"Yes, my vicar." Belam's tone was quite calm. For decades he had been a Defender of the Faith and a Prince of the Temple. From close range he had seen them come and go, and he was not easily perturbed by vicarial tempers.

Nabur felt the need to explain. "Belam, it is *needful* that we be shown increased respect. The infidels and heretics are tearing apart the world which has been given by God into our care!" The last sentence came bursting out, a cry from the inner heart.

"My faith is firm, my Vicar, that our prayers and our armies will yet prevail."

"Prevail?" The vicar came stalking toward him, grimacing sarcastically. "Of course! Someday. Before the end of time! But *now*, Belam, *now* our Holy Temple lies bleeding and suffering, and we . . ." The vicarial voice dropped temporarily into almost inaudible weakness. "We must bear many burdens. Many and heavy, Belam. You cannot begin to realize, until you mount our throne."

Belam bowed, in sincere and silent reverence.

The vicar paced again, skirts flapping. This time he had a goal. From his high-piled worktable he snatched up in shaking fist a pamphlet that was already worn from handling, and wrinkled, as if it had perhaps been once or twice crumpled up and thrown across a room.

Belam knew what the pamphlet was. A contributing if not a sufficient cause of today's rage, he thought, with his cool habit of theologian's logic. A small thorn compared with others. But this particular barb had stabbed Nabur in the tenderest part of his vanity.

Nabur was shaking the paper-covered booklet at him.

"Because you have been away, Belam, we have not yet had the opportunity to discuss with you this—this back-stabbing abomination of Messire Vincento's! This so-called *Dialogue on the Movement of the Tides*! Have you read it?"

"I—"

"The wretched man cares nothing about the tides. In this pamphlet his purpose is to once more promulgate his heresy-tainted dreams. He clings to his wish to reduce the solid world beneath our feet to a mere speck, to send us all flying around the sun. But even that is not enough. No, not for him!"

Belam frowned now in real puzzlement. "What else, my Vicar?"

Nabur advanced on him in a glow of anger, as if the Defender were the guilty one. "What else? I will tell you! The arguments of this pamphlet are cast in the form of a debate among three persons. And Vincento its author intends one of these fictional debaters—the one who defends traditional ideas, who therefore is described as 'simple-minded' and 'below the level of human intelligence'—he intends this person to represent ourself!"

"My Vicar!"

Nabur nodded vigorously. "Oh, yes. Some of our very words are put into the mouth of this simpleton, so-called!"

Belam was shaking his head in strong doubt. "Vincento has never been moderate in his disputes, which have been many. Many? Nay, continuous, rather. But I am convinced that he has not in this pamphlet or elsewhere intended any irreverence, either to your person or to your holy office."

"I know what he intended here!" Vicar Nabur almost screamed the words. Then the most honored man in the world—possibly also the most hated, quite possibly also the most burdened by what he saw as his God-given tasks—

groaned incontinently and, like a spoiled child, threw himself into a chair.

Arrogance remained, as always, but the spoiled-child aspect did not last long. Irascible humors having been discharged, calm and intelligence returned.

"Belam."

"My Vicar?"

"Have you yet had time to study this pamphlet, while on your travels perhaps? I know it has been widely circulated."

Belam gravely inclined his head.

"Then give us your considered opinion."

"I am a theologian, my Vicar, and not a natural philosopher. Therefore I have taken counsel with astronomers and others and find my own opinion in this matter generally confirmed. Which is that Vincento's arguments in this pamphlet concerning the tides really prove nothing regarding the movement of the celestial bodies, and are not even very accurate as regards the tides themselves."

"He thinks we are all fools, to be dazzled by brilliant words into accepting whatever shoddy logic he offers us. And that we will not even realize it when we are mocked!" The vicar stood up for a moment, sighed, and then tiredly resumed his seat.

Belam chose to ignore the theory, which he did not for a moment believe, that the pamphlet's aim was sacrilegious mockery. The real issue was vital enough. "As the vicar may possibly recall, I had occasion some years ago to write to Vincento regarding his speculations on the idea of a sun-centered universe. Then, as now, such theorizing caused me concern in my capacity as Defender."

"We recall the occasion very well, ha hum. In fact, Messire Vincento has already been summoned here to stand trial for his violation in this pamphlet of your injunction at that time. . . . Belam, what were the precise words of your warning, again?''

Belam thought awhile before answering, and then spoke slowly and precisely. "I wrote him, first, that mathematicians are quite free to calculate and publish whatever they wish regarding the celestial appearances or any other natural phenomena—provided they remain strictly in the realm of hypothesis.

"Secondly, it is quite a different matter to say that *in fact* the sun is in the center of the universe. That *in fact* our globe spins from west to east each day, while revolving round the sun each year. Such statements must be considered very dangerous; though not formally heretical, they are liable to injure faith by contradicting the Holy Writings."

"Your memory, Belam, is even more than usually excellent. Just when did you write this letter of injunction?"

"Fifteen years ago, my Vicar." Belam showed a dry smile momentarily. "Though I must admit that I re-read our archive copy this morning."

He was utterly serious again. "Thirdly and lastly, I wrote Vincento that if some real proof existed of the sun-centered universe he champions, we should then be forced to revise our interpretations of those passages in the Holy Writings which would appear to say otherwise. We have in the past revised our scriptural interpretations, for example in regard to the roundness of the world. But, in the absence of any such proof, the weight of authority and traditional opinion is not to be set aside."

Nabur was listening with great attentiveness. "It seems to us, Belam, that you wrote well, as usual."

"Thank you, my Vicar."

Satisfaction appeared mixed with anger in the vicarial mien. "In this pamphlet Vincento has certainly violated your injunction! The debater into whose mouth he puts his own opinions advances no convincing proofs, at least none that can be grasped by mere mortals like ourselves. And yet he does argue, at great length, that in very truth our globe spins like a toy top beneath our feet. To convince the reader of this is his plain intention. Then!'' The vicar stood up, dramatically. ''Then, on the last page, *our* argument—often expressed by us as a means of compromising these difficult philosophical matters—*our* argument, that God may produce whatever effect He likes in the world, without being bound by scientific causes—*our* argument is quoted by the simpleton-debater who has been wrong about everything else; quoted as coming from 'a person of high learning and wisdom, supremely above contradiction.' And at this the other debaters piously declare themselves silenced and decide to adjourn for refreshment. One cannot fail to see them, and their author, laughing up their sleeves!''

While the vicar struggled to regain his breath and calm once more, there was silence in the apartment, save for the workmen's shouts and laughter drifting in. What were they doing out there? Oh, yes, only the marble. Belam uttered a brief prayer that he might never again be required to order a stake prepared for a heretic.

When Nabur spoke again, it was in a reasonable tone. ''Now, Belam. Other than this weary argument on tides, which all seem to agree is inconclusive, do you suppose there can exist anywhere any evidence for Vincento's spinning world? Anything he might impertinently introduce at his trial to . . . disrupt its course?''

Belam drew himself up, slightly but perceptibly. ''My Vicar, we shall of course conduct Vincento's trial, or any other, with the greatest zeal for the truth that we can muster. Vincento may argue in his own defense—''

''Of course, of course!'' Nabur interrupted with a rapid dismissive waving of his hand; it was the gesture he used at a time when another man might apologize. But then he still waited for an answer.

After frowning thoughtfully at the floor, Belam began to give what a later age would call a background briefing. "My Vicar, I have through the years made an effort to keep abreast of astronomers' thinking. I fear many of them, religious and laymen both, have become Messire Vincento's enemies. He has a relish and skill for making others look like fools. He has arrogance, in claiming for his own all that these new devices, telescopes, discover in the heavens. An arrogant and argumentative man is hard to bear, and triply hard when he is so often in the right." Belam glanced up sharply for a moment, but Nabur had not taken the description as applying to anyone but Vincento. "My Vicar, is it not true that this pamphlet was brought to your attention by some priest-astronomer whom Vincento has offended and bested in some debate?" Though Belam knew of a number of such men, he was really only guessing.

"Hum. It may be so, Belam, it may be so. But Vincento's offense is real, though it may have been maliciously called to our attention."

The two of them were pacing now, with old men's measured tread, sometimes orbiting each other like perturbed planets. The Defender of the Faith said, "I raise the point to show the difficulty of obtaining unbiased testimony in this matter from other scholars. They are certainly unlikely to rush to Vincento's defense. Nevertheless, I believe that most astronomers now perform their calculations using the mathematical assumption that the planets, or some of them, at least, revolve about the sun. Of course, that idea is not original with Vincento, nor is the idea that our globe is only a planet. It seems these assumptions make the mathematics of celestial movement more elegant and somewhat more satisfying to the scholar; fewer epicycles need be included in the orbits to make them fit the circular form—"

"Yes, yes, Vincento makes the mathematics more elegant. But stick to the point. Can he have *proof*, mathematical or otherwise? Plain evidence of any kind?"

"I would say rather the contrary."

"Ha!" Nabur stopped pacing and faced Belam squarely, almost smiling.

The Defender said, "Had Vincento any plain proof, I think he would have printed it here. And there *is* solid evidence against him." Belam gestured with his scholar's hands, frail fingers unsure of technicalities but still grasping firmly whatever they were required to grasp. "It seems that if our globe did make a yearly journey round the sun, the relative positions of the fixed stars should appear to us to change from month to month, as we approached certain constellations or drew away from them. And no such displacement of the stars can be observed."

Vicar Nabur was nodding, looking satisfied.

Belam made a shrugging gesture. "Of course, it is possible to argue that the stars are simply too distant for our measurements to discover such displacement. Vincento will always have arguments, if he wants to use them. . . . I fear that no other astronomer is going to be able to prove him wrong, much as some of them would love to do so. No, I think we must admit that the celestial appearances would be essentially the same if we *did* go round the sun."

"That is enough for any reasonable man to say."

"Exactly, my Vicar. As I wrote Vincento, where there is lack of other certainty, we have no excuse for turning our backs on tradition and substituting strained interpretations for the plain meaning of the Holy Writings." Belam's voice was rising gradually, achieving the tone of power that it would have in court. "We of the Temple have the solemn duty before God to uphold the truth that those

Writings reveal. And, my Vicar, what I wrote to Vincento fifteen years ago is still true today—I have never been shown any proof of the motion of the world we stand on, and so I cannot believe that any such proof or any such motion exists!''

The vicar had resumed his seat. Now his face was gentle, as he raised his hands, then clamped them down decisively on the arms of his ornate work-chair. ''Then it is our decision that you and the other Defenders must proceed with the trial.'' Nabur spoke regretfully at first, though as he went on his anger gradually returned, less vehement than it had been. ''We do not doubt that he can be convicted of violating your injunction. But understand, we have no wish to visit any great punishment upon our erring son.''

Belam bowed his grateful assent to that.

Nabur went on, ''In charity we grant that he intended no attack upon the Faith and no insult to our person. He is only headstrong, and stubborn, and intemperate in debate. And sadly lacking in gratitude and humility! He must be taught that he *cannot* set himself up as a superior authority on all matters temporal and spiritual. . . . Did he not once attempt to lecture *you* on theology?''

Belam once more inclined his head in assent, meanwhile sharply warning himself that he must guard against taking any personal satisfaction in Vincento's approaching humiliation.

Even now Nabur could not let the subject drop, not yet. ''Ah, I could curse the man! In the past, we ourself have been among the first to heap praise on his achievements. We have granted him hours of private audience. We have shown him friendliness to a degree we do not always extend to princes! Before ascending to this chair, we ourself once even wrote a pamphlet in his praise! And now, how are we repaid?''

''I understand, my Vicar.''

*   *   *

"I see you have requested assignment to one particular time, Colonel Odegard." Colonel Lukas spoke the words around his cigar, while at the same time using the formal style of address. He was a sometime drinking acquaintance of Derron's, who might be finding it a little difficult to strike the right balance in his role today of examining psychologist. If he had been a close friend of Derron's he would probably have disqualified himself as examiner. But what close friends did Derron have these days among the living? There was Chan Amling . . . an old classmate, yes. Bosom buddy, no. The fact was that he had none.

Lukas was looking at him. "Yes, I did," Derron answered, somewhat tardily.

Lukas shifted his cigar. "The two days Vincento spends near the town of Oibbog, delayed on his way to his trial. Waiting to cross a flooded river. Had you any particular reason for wanting that time?"

Oh, yes, he had. He had not put it into words, however, even for himself, and was not about to try to do so now. "Just that I know the locale very well. I once spent a long holiday there. It was one of those places that didn't change very much in three or four hundred years." Of course, the town and cathedral of Oibbog, like all the other surface landmarks of the planet, were now in the past tense. Derron's particular reason was that the long holiday there had been with *her*. He caught himself sliding forward tensely on his chair again and forced himself to slump a little and relax.

Squinting through his cigar smoke, Colonel Lukas shuffled uncertainly through the papers on his desk and then threw one of his sneaky fast balls. "Have you any particular reason for wanting to be an agent at all?"

For Derron that question immediately called up an image of Matt and Ay, two forms blending more and more into a single kingly figure as they receded from the moving moment of the present. Their heroic image seemed to be growing steadily larger with distance, the way a mountain in the old days on the surface had sometimes seemed to swell as you hiked away from it.

But that was not the sort of reason a man could talk about; at least not without all of a sudden sounding far too noble and dedicated.

Derron made himself slide back in his chair again. "Well, as I said, I know the period very well. I believe I can do a good job. Like everyone else, I want to win the war." He was uttering noble sentiments after all, and too many of them. Better stretch it into a joke. "I want prestige, I suppose. Accomplishment. Promotion. You name it. Did I hit the right one yet?"

"What is the right one?" Lukas shrugged glumly. "I don't know why I'm required to ask that—why does anyone want to be an agent?" He shaped his papers into a neat stack before him. "Now, Colonel. Just one more thing I want to bring up before certifying you as good agent material. That is the matter of your personal religious views."

"I'm not religious."

"How do you feel *about* religion?"

Relax, relax. "Well, frankly, I think that gods and temples are fine things for people who need crutches. I haven't yet found any necessary."

"I see. I think this is a valid psychological point which should be raised, because there are dangers inherent in sending back to Vincento's time anyone who is likely to find himself susceptible to ideological fever." Lukas made an apologetic gesture. "You as an historian understand better than I how thick dogmas and doctrines are in the air back there. Religious and philosophical controversy seems to draw all the energy of that era."

"Yes." Derron nodded. "I see what you mean. You don't want a fanatic of any stripe. Well, I'm not what they call a militant atheist. My conscience will let me play any part that's necessary." Maybe he was explaining too much, talking too much, but he had to make this point, he had to be allowed to go. "I'll be a rabid monk and spit on Vincento if required."

"I don't suppose Time Ops will ask that of you. All right, then, Derron. You're in."

And Derron tried not to show too much relief.

What Operations really decided was that he would do best in the part of a traveling scholar. They gave him a name—Valzay—and started to build for him an identity that had never historically existed. He was supposedly from Mosnar, a country distant from Vincento's but for the most part faithful to the Holy Temple. Valzay was to be one of the itinerant intellectuals of Vincento's time, who wandered somewhat like sacred cows across minor political and language boundaries, from one university or wealthy patron to another.

Derron and a dozen other chosen agents, mostly male, were rushed into preparation. Working singly or in pairs, they were to keep Vincento under practically continuous observation during the now doubly critical days of his life just preceding his trial and during it. Each agent or team would remain on the job for a day or two and then be relieved by another. Chan Amling, now a captain, was assigned as Derron's team partner; they would not often be together on the job, but would alternate in keeping Vincento more or less in sight. Amling was to play the role of one of the wandering friars who in Vincento's day were quite numerous, and for the most part only loosely disciplined.

The program of preparation was hurried and rugged, beginning with the surgical implantation of communications transducers in jawbone and skull. This would enable each agent to remain in contact with Operations without having to mumble aloud or wear anything as bulky as a helmet.

There were speech and manners to be rehearsed, some knowledge of events current in Vincento's day to be memorized, and some knowledge to be repressed, of events in the immediate future of that time. There were the techniques of communications and weaponry to be mastered—all this in a few days.

Amid his fatigue and concentration, Derron noticed almost without surprise that Lisa was now working in Operations, one of the calm-voiced girls who relayed orders and information to individual sentries and could do the same for slave-unit operators, or for live agents when some of them took the field.

He had only scraps of free time now and made no effort to use any of it to speak to her. The knowledge that he was on his way back to Oibbog had crowded almost everything else out of his mind. He felt like a man going to a rendezvous with his own true love; the people of flesh and blood around him, Lisa included, took on the semblance of shadows for him even as the dead past grew more vivid.

Then one day, as he and Amling sat in folding chairs at the side of Stage Three, resting between behavior drills, Lisa came walking past and stopped.

"Derron, I want to wish you success."

"Thanks. Pull up a chair, if you like."

She did. Amling decided he wanted to stretch his legs, and he ambled away.

Lisa said, "Derron, I shouldn't have accused you of killing Matt. I know you didn't want him to die, that you felt as bad as I did about it. What happened to him wasn't your fault." She was speaking like someone who had lost a friend among other friends in war. Not like someone whose life had been destroyed with the life of her beloved. "I've just been mastering my own internal difficulties—you know about that—but that's no excuse for what I said. I should have known you better. I'm sorry."

"It's all right." Derron shifted uncomfortably in his chair, sorry that she felt so bad about it. "Really, it's . . . Lisa, I thought you and I might have had—something. I suppose not the whole thing there can be between a man and a woman, but still something good."

She looked away from him, a faint frown creasing her forehead. "I had some feeling like that about Matt. But that much of a feeling would never be enough for me."

He went on hurriedly. "As far as anything permanent and tremendous is concerned, well, I've tried that already, once in my life. And I'm still up to my neck in it, as you may have noticed. I'm sorry, I've got to get moving." And he jumped up out of his chair and hurried to where Amling and the others were not yet ready for him.

When the day came for the drop, the costumers dressed Derron in clothing that was slightly worn but good, suitable for a fairly successful gentleman-scholar on his travels far from home. In his haversack they placed a reasonable supply of food, along with a flask of brandy. Into his wallet went a moderate sum of the proper coins, silver and gold, and also a forged letter of credit on an Empire City bank. They hoped he would not need much money, and plans did not call for him to get to within a hundred miles of the Holy City. But just in case.

Chan Amling was issued a somewhat worn and soiled gray friar's habit, but very little else, in keeping with his mendicant role. He did half-seriously request permission to take along a pair of dice, arguing that he would not be the first friar in history to go so armed. But Time Ops was soon able to establish that such equipment was scarcely standard issue for religious, even in Vincento's time, and he turned down the request.

Both Derron and Chan had hung around their necks abominably carved wooden wedge-symbols. The images differed in detail of design, but each was big enough to conceal the bulk of a miniaturized communicator, as well as being too ugly and cheap-looking for anyone to want to steal. If any of Vincento's contemporaries should be moved to wonder audibly why Derron wore such a thing, he was to say that it was a present from his wife.

From an arsenal assembled in Stage Three, Odegard and Amling were issued sturdy travelers' staffs. These again were dissimilar in outer detail, but both were much more effective weapons than they appeared to be. All of the agents were armed, with staffs or other innocent-appearing devices; they were all to be dropped within half a minute of one another, present-time, though, of course, they were to arrive in different places and on different days.

Their processing for this mission had been too hurried and with too much individual attention for them to get to know one another very well. But during the last few minutes before the drop, as the masquerade-costumed group bade one another good luck and good berserker hunting, there was an atmosphere of joking camaraderie in Stage Three.

Derron felt it. It crossed his mind that once again he had good friends among the living. The launching file formed on order, and he took his place in it calmly, looking forward over short Chan Amling's gray-cowled head.

Amling turned his head slightly. "Five will get you ten," he whispered, "that I land up to my crotch in mud someplace. Out of sight of the bloody road, at least."

"No bet," said Derron automatically, as the count began. The line moved briskly forward, one figure after another in front of him abruptly vanishing from his sight.

Amling made some last remark that Derron could not catch, and then Amling too was gone.

It was Derron's turn. He swung a booted foot in a long stride out over the mercurial launching circle, then brought it down.

He was standing in darkness, and around him was the unmistakable, never-to-be-forgotten feeling of open air. Except for a mere whisper of breeze and a drizzle of rain, he was immersed in an echoless silence, a great loneliness in which his materialization must have passed unnoticed. Good.

"Reverend Brother?" he inquired of the darkness in a low voice, speaking in Vincento's language. There was no answer; Amling might well have come down in some mud hole out of sight of the road. He had a knack for achieving what he was willing to bet on.

As Derron's eyes grew more accustomed to the gloom, he realized that the hard surface under his own boots did indeed seem to be the stones of the old Empire highway that passed through Oibbog. Operations had put at least half of the team spatially on the bull's-eye, then. Whether they had done as well temporally remained to be seen, though rain and darkness were reassuring signs.

Subvocalizing, Derron tried to reach Operations for a routine check-in, but the communicator seemed utterly dead. Some kind of paradox-loop would be blocking contact. Such things cropped up now and then; there was nothing to do but hope that the condition would not last long.

He waited the agreed-upon few minutes for Amling, meanwhile opening his staff at one end and consulting the compass thus revealed, to make sure of the direction he was facing on the road. Then, after calling once more to his reverend brother with no result, he began to walk, boots clopping solidly on the pavement. Lightning flashed distantly at irregular intervals. He drank deep breaths of the washed air.

He had not gone far before the transducer behind his ear gave him a sudden twinge. ". . . Odegard, can you read me yet? Colonel Odegard . . ." The male voice sounded weary and bored.

"This is Colonel Odegard; I read you."

"Colonel!" Sudden excitement. Off mike: "We've got contact, sir!" Back on: "Colonel, it's plus two days and three hours here since you were dropped. Time scale has been slipping."

"Understand." Derron kept his speech subvocal. "I'm about plus five minutes since dropping. Still on the road in the rain, at night. No contact with Amling yet."

"Odegard, you're blurring on the screens." It was Time Ops' voice speaking now. "But it looks like you're farther from the cathedral than we intended, just about two miles. You may be outside the safety zone, so get in closer to Vincento as fast as possible." By "safety zone," of course, Time Ops meant the zone of protection against any direct violence from the berserker, a zone created by the intense concentration of sentry observation round Vincento's lifeline. "We've just pulled out the team ahead of you. They report all's well with Vincento. You say you haven't seen Amling yet."

"Right." Derron stepped up his pace a trifle, though he was having to tap along with his staff to be sure of not floundering off the pavement into the mud.

"We haven't found him either. Can't see his line in this blurring on the screens. It may be just the time-slippage and a paradox-loop."

Lightning flared directly ahead of Derron, obligingly showing him that his road ran straight for some distance in that direction and giving him a glimpse of the cathedral spire, which was farther off than it should have been. He supposed it was about two miles away.

He reported this to Operations, meanwhile puzzling over something else that the lightning had shown him—a dully gleaming object in the center of the road ahead, lying atop a line or thin trench that seemed to have been scratched or dug across the pavement.

". . . I'm just coming up to it now. Looks like . . ."

It was soft to the prodding tip of his staff. He waited for the lightning, which flashed again in a few seconds.

"Never mind trying to contact Amling anymore." The body was quite naked; it could have been here a day or an hour. Derron stood over it, describing the situation as best he could. Human robbers might have stolen a staff and even a cheap pectoral wedge, but would they have taken a friar's habit? . . .

He bent to touch the deep scratch mark that cut across the road beneath the body. No medieval tool had made that ruler-straight slice through stone; quite likely it had been carved by the same cybernetic limb that had removed the back of Amling's head.

"Ops, I think it's marked the boundary of the safety zone for us. To let us know that it knows about it."

"Yes, yes, you may be right, Odegard, but never mind that now. You just move in close to Vincento quickly. Protect yourself."

He was moving that way already, walking backward and holding his staff like a rifle while all his senses probed as best they could the rainy night through which he had just passed. Not that all his alertness would do him any good, if the enemy was out there and able to strike.

But Derron lived. After a hundred paces he turned and walked normally ahead, once more making good time. The berserker had killed casually, in passing, leaving its mark like some defiant human outlaw. And then it had gone on to its more pressing business here.

By the time Derron had reached the place where the road bent sharply to the left toward the washed-out bridge, the lightning had gone on over the horizon; he felt rather than saw the bulk of the hill and its cathedral ahead of him and above. But nearer, close by the side of the road, he could make out the monastery's high wall, the tumbled stones of what had been an arched gateway, and the remnants of a broken gate. And when he stood just before the gateway he could distinguish, just inside, a coach that he knew must be Vincento's; standing deserted in a puddle. From the shelter of a cloister came the gentle mumbling and grunting of load-beasts. Derron paused only a moment before plodding on through the gate and across a soggy garth toward what looked like the main entrance of the main building, which was a sprawling one-story structure.

He made no effort to be quiet, and the dark doorway before him promptly emitted a challenge. "Who's there? Stand and give your name!"

The dialect was one that Derron had expected to run into. He stopped in his tracks and, as the beam of a lantern flicked out at him, he answered. "I am Valzay of Mosnar, mathematicus and scholar. From the coach and animals I see here, I judge that you within are honest men. And I have need of shelter."

"Step for'ard then," said the wary male voice that had challenged him. A door cracked, and behind the door the lantern retreated.

Derron advanced slowly, displaying hands empty save for an innocent staff. When he had gotten in out of the rain, the door was shut behind him, and the lantern brightened. He found himself in what must have been the com-

mon room of the monastery. Facing him stood a pair of
soldiers, one armed with a crude pistol and the other with
a short sword; judging by their patchwork uniforms, they
were members of one of the mercenary companies that were
now multiplying in this war-torn land.

When they could see his gentleman's clothes more plainly,
the soldiers' manner became more or less respectful. "Well,
sir, how d'you come to be awanderin' afoot and alone?"

He scowled and swore, wringing water from his cloak.
He related how his skittish load-beast, scared by lightning,
had run off with his light sulky. A plague was too good for
that animal! If he could catch it in the morning, he'd have
some of its hide off in narrow strips, they could bet on
that! With whip-cracking vehemence he shook water from
his broad-brimmed hat.

Derron had an effortless feel and skill for acting when
there was a need for it, and these lines had been well
rehearsed. The soldiers chuckled, relaxed most of their
vigilance, and became willing to chat. There was, they
said, plenty of room for another boarder here, because the
proprietary monks had all cleared out long ago. The place
was no tavern with girls and ale, worse luck, and even
firewood was in short supply, but the roof did keep the
rain off. Yes, they were from a mercenary company, one
that was now in the pay of the Holy Temple. Their
captain, with the bulk of his men, was now in Oibbog
across the river.

"And if the cap'n can't do no more'n wave to us for
the next couple days, why that's all right with us, hey
what?"

For all the jocularity, they still maintained a minimal
professional suspicion of Derron—he might conceivably
be a scout for some well-organized band of brigands—and
so they did not tell him how many soldiers had been
caught on this side of the torrent when the bridge they had

been guarding collapsed. He did not ask, of course, but he gathered there were not many.

In answer to a question he did ask, one of the soldiers said, "Naw, no one but the old gentleman as owns the coach, and his servant an' his driver. And a pair o' friars. Plenty empty cells, sir, so take your pick. One's about as damp as the next."

Derron murmured his thanks and then, with some brief assistance from the lantern, groped his way down a vaulted passage lined with doorless cells and into one of these, which was pointed out to him as unoccupied. Built against the cell's rear wall was a wooden bunk frame that had not yet been ripped out for firewood. Derron sat down to pull off his squelching boots, while the lantern's light receded once more down the passage and vanished.

His boots off and tipped to drain, Derron stretched out on the wooden frame, the knapsack under his head, a dry garment from the knapsack over him for cover, his staff within easy reach. He did not yet have the feeling of having achieved his goal and returned to Oibbog. Amling's death seemed a bit unreal. Neither could he quite grasp the fact that Vincent Vincento in the living flesh was somewhere within a few meters of him, that one of the founding fathers of the Modern world might even be the author of the snore that now drifted faintly down the passage.

Lying on his wooden bed, Derron reported briefly to Operations, bringing them up to the minute on his progress so far; then, genuinely tired, he found himself drifting toward sleep. The sound of rain was lulling, and there was nothing he could do about getting a look at Vincento until the morning. Even as his consciousness dulled, it struck him as mildly odd that his thoughts were occupied neither with his mission for Operations nor his private mission of return. Not with the staggering fact of time travel, or the loss of Amling, or the menace of the berserker. Simply with the fading sound of diminishing rain and the freshness of the infinite clean atmosphere around him. It was the theme of resurrection. . . .

He was jarred out of the beginning of sleep when Operations put a throbbing behind his right ear. He came wide awake at once, with only a mild start, and tucked his carven wedge-symbol closer under his chin.

"Odegard, we're starting to read through some of this blurring on the screens. We can count fourteen lifelines in or near that monastery-temple complex. One of them, of course, is your own. Another is Vincento's. Another one seems to be an unborn child's line; you know how they show on a screen in dots and dashes."

Derron shifted his position slightly on the creaking wooden rack; he felt oddly comfortable and snug, hearing the last dripping of the rain outside. He mused subvocally, "Let's see. Me, Vincento, his two servants, and the two soldiers I've seen. That makes six. And they said there were two friars. Eight, which would leave six more unaccounted for. Probably four more soldiers and a camp follower who's picked up a little dotted line she won't want to carry. Wait a minute, though—that one soldier did say something about there being no girls here. Anyway, I suppose your idea is that one of the apparent people I find here will have no lifeline showing on your screens—meaning he or she is really our hypothetical berserker-android."

"That's our idea, yes."

"Tomorrow I can count noses and . . . Wait."

In the darkness of the entrance to Derron's cell, a shape of lesser blackness became discrete with movement. The figure of a hooded friar, utterly faceless in the gloom, came a half-step into the cell before halting abruptly.

Derron froze, recalling the hooded robe missing from Amling's corpse. His hand moved to his staff and gripped it tightly. But he would not dare to use his weaponry

without being very sure of his target. Even then, at this
close range, the staff would be torn from his hands and
broken before he could aim it. . . .

Only an instant had passed since the hooded figure had
entered. Now it muttered a few indistinguishable words,
which might have been an apology for entering the wrong
cell. And in another moment it had withdrawn into the
blackness, as noiselessly as it had come.

Derron remained half-risen on one elbow, still gripping
his useless weapon. He told Operations what had just
happened.

"It won't dare kill you there, remember. Be very sure
before you fire."

"Understand." Slowly he stretched out again. But all
comfort had gone with the last of the rain, and resurrection
was a lie.

When Vincento was awakened by a touch, and found
himself in darkness, bedded amid damp straw with bare
stone walls close about him, he knew a moment of sinking
terror. The worst had already happened, and he lay in the
Defenders' dungeon. The terror was deepened when he
saw the faceless monk-hooded figure bending over him.
He could see it by the moonlight which now filtered
through the tiny window—evidently the rain was over. . . .

The rain . . . Of course, he was still on his way to the
Holy City, his trial was still to come! The intensity of his
relief was such that Vincento accepted almost with courtesy his being awakened. "What do you want?" he muttered, sitting up on his shelf of a bed and pulling his
traveling-rug closer about his shoulders. His manservant
Will slept on, a huddled mound on the dark floor.

The visitor's hooded face could not be seen. The visitor's voice was a sepulchral whisper. "Messire Vincento,
you are to come alone to the cathedral tomorrow morning.

At the crossways of nave and transepts you will receive good news from your friends in high places.''

He tried to digest this. Could it be that Nabur or perhaps Belam wanted to send him some secret reassurance of leniency? That was possible. More likely, this was some Defenders' trickery. A man summoned to trial was not supposed to discuss the matter with anyone.

"It will be good news, Messire Vincento. Come alone, and be willing to wait if you are not met at once. The crossways of nave and transepts. And do not seek to learn my name or see my face.''

Vincento maintained his silence, determined to commit himself to nothing. And his visitor, satisfied that the message had been delivered, melted away into the night.

When Vincento awakened the next time, it was from a pleasant dream. He had been back in his own villa, on the estate that had been provided for him by the senate of his city, safe in his own bed with his mistress's warm body solid and comforting beside him. In reality the woman had been gone for some time—women no longer meant very much—but the estate was still there. If only they would let him return to it in peace!

This time he had been aroused by a touch of a different sort—the touch on his face of a shaft of morning sunlight, which came striking into his cell from the high thin window of the cell across the corridor. As he lay recalling with curiosity his strange midnight visitor, making sure in his own mind that *that* had been no dream, the sun shaft was already moving slowly away from his face. And instantly that motion made it a golden pendulum of subtle torture, driving all other thoughts from his mind.

The pendulum he really faced was that of choice. His mind could swing one way, *tick,* and meet in foresight the shame of swallowed truth and swallowed pride, all the humiliation of an enforced recanting. And if he swung his thoughts the other way, *tock*, there they confronted the breaking agony of the boot or the rack or the slower destruction in a buried cell.

It was not a dozen years since the Defenders had burned Onadroig alive in the Great Square of the Holy City. Of course Onadroig had been no scientist, but rather a poet and a philosopher. The consensus these days among scholars was that he must have also been a madman, an utter fanatic who had walked into a fire rather than give over his theories. And what theories had possessed him! He had believed that the Holy One had been no more than a magician; that the chief of devils would one day be saved; that there were infinite worlds in space, that the very stars were peopled.

Neither in the Scriptures nor in nature could the least justification for any of these absurd ideas be found—so Belam and the other Defenders had argued, indefatigably but fruitlessly trying to change Onadroig's mind during the seven years' imprisonment that had preceded his burning as an incorrigible heretic.

To Vincento himself, the crude physical torture was a remote threat only. He or any other reputable scholar would have to show very deliberate and prolonged stubbornness before the Defenders would employ any such methods against him. But the threat would be in the background, all the same. At his trial he would be formally threatened with torture, perhaps even shown the instruments. All ritual, no more. But it was not possible that it should come to that. *They* would say, with genuine unhappiness, that a defendant who absolutely refused to yield to all milder methods of persuasion forced them to take harsh measures, for the good of his immortal soul and the protection of the Faith.

So—his pendulum of choice was imaginary. He had no

real choice but to recant. Let the sun move any way they wanted it to. Let it go whirling around the globe in an insane yearly spiral, to please the arrogant, short-sighted fools who thought they had already read all the secrets of the universe in a few dusty pages of the Holy Writings.

Lying on his back, Vincento raised a hand veined with ropy vessels against the slow-swiveling torture blade of the sun. But the sun would not be stopped in its motion by any man's hand. It mocked him all the more, making bright translucent wax of the old bones and flesh of his fingers.

On the floor, Will stirred sluggishly in his rug cocoon. Vincento barked him awake and chased him outside to rouse the coachman, Rudd, who slept beside the beasts— Rudd to look at the river's level, Will to make some tea and get a little food ready for breakfast. Vincento had had the foresight to provision his coach well.

Left alone, he began the slow humiliating process of getting his aging bones unlimbered and ready for what the day might bring. In recent years his health had been poor, and now each day began with a cautious testing of sensation. But he was not sick now, only old. And, yes, he was afraid.

By the time Will came to inform him that a fire and hot tea were ready in the monastery's common room, Vincento was ready to step forth. Somewhat to his surprise, he discovered when he entered the common room that another wayfarer had arrived during the night, a youngster who introduced himself as Valzay of the distant land of Mosnar.

Valzay, as he put it himself, made a modest claim to scholarship. Hearing this, Vincento studied him more carefully. But, for a wonder, the youngster was decently respectful, seeming to regard Vincento with genuine if restrained awe, and murmuring that even in his distant homeland Vincento's discoveries were known and praised.

Vincento acknowledged all this with pleased nods, mean-

while sipping his breakfast tea and wondering if this youth
was the bearer of the good news he was supposed to hear
this morning from someone in the cathedral. *Might* it after
all be a word of hope from Nabur? He scowled. No, he
would not let himself hope, like a vassal, for another
man's kindness, not even when the other was the Vicar of
the Holy One himself. He straightened his back. Anyway,
he was not going to rush up the hill to the temple at once.

Rudd came to report that the river was no longer rising,
but was still too high and dangerous for anyone to think of
trying to ford it here. In one more day it would probably
be safe.

So Vincento took his time at finishing his tea and con-
suming a little food. He left word with Rudd to take some
food to the two friars and then strolled leisurely out into
the sunshine to warm his bones. If he came late to his trial,
there were plenty of witnesses here to tell the reason. Let
the Defenders inveigh against the river, if they liked. No
doubt the torrent, in deference to their superior knowledge
of the Holy Writings, would dry up. No doubt all of nature
would do their bidding; it was likely the ruined bridge here
would rebuild itself if they came to threaten the stones of
torture.

But no, away with such thoughts; he must begin to
practice his humility. He called to Will to fetch him his
writing materials from the coach and then he went out
through the broken gate to sit alone in the sun beside the
road, with one tumbled block of stone for a bench and
another for a table. He might as well put his time to use,
start writing his statement of recantation to present during
the trial.

Of course, the accused was not supposed to know why
he had been summoned. Probably the Defenders' first
question would be whether or not he had any idea of what
he had been charged with. No doubt such an opening

sometimes brought unsuspected crimes bursting to light from guilty lips, but in Vincento's case there could hardly be any doubt of the reason for his summons. It had been fifteen years since Belam's warning injunction, which Vincento himself had since managed almost to forget. Other scholars before and since had talked of the heliocentric hypothesis with impunity and had used it in their published calculations. But when the Defenders' summons came, Vincento realized that he had bitterly antagonized men who were in high places and who never forgot anything.

The first paper he pulled from his portable escritoire was the old letter of injunction from Defender Belam. Involuntarily, Vincento's eye went at once to the words, "no proof of our globe's motion exists, as I believe, since none has been shown to me."

No proof. Vincento wiped at his forehead with a tremulous hand. Now, with mortal fear to enforce bleak clarity of thought, he could see that the arguments he had conjured from tides and sunspots really proved nothing at all about the motions of sun and planets. The truth about those motions had become apparent to him before he had ever thought of the need for proving it. He had looked long through telescopes and he had thought long and deeply about what he saw. With eyes and mind he had weighed the sun, he had grasped at stars and planets and comets, and truth had come through some inward door, like a revelation.

His enemies who cried him down were, of course, far lesser men than he. They were stupid and blind in their refusal, or their inability, to see what he showed them as the truth. And yet he knew that those who were to sit as his judges were shrewd enough logicians when they set themselves to think within their formal rules. If only there were some firm proof, simple and incontrovertible, that he might set before them . . . oh, what would he not give for that! His mind ached, his fists clenched, his very guts contracted at the thought. If he had one solid simple proof he would risk all, he would dare anything, to confront and confound his enemies with it, to rub their long arrogant noses in the truth!

But since in fact he had nothing to support this mood of glorious defiance, it soon passed. The truth was, he was old and afraid and he was going to recant.

Slowly he got out pen and ink and blank paper; slowly he began his first draft. From time to time he paused, sitting with closed eyes in the sun, trying not to think.

Derron counted seven soldiers around the breakfast fire, and he found each of them overjoyed to accept a swallow of brandy from his traveling flask and willing enough to talk. No, there was no one he had not seen in the monastery or the cathedral, or anywhere nearer than the town across the river. Not that they knew of, and they would know.

When he was alone in the privy a few minutes later, Derron did some subvocal mumbling. "Operations?"

"Time Ops here."

Maybe the Commander never had to sleep, but Derron himself was sufficiently tired and strained to dispense with military courtesy. "Count the lifelines here again. I make it just thirteen of us. If you can make it twelve, then one of my smiling companions has clockwork for guts. But if you come out with *fourteen* again, then either there's some bandit or deserter lurking in a corner I haven't seen or you're misreading your screens. I think that dotted line at least is a mistake in interpretation; I consider it unlikely that any of us here is pregnant, since we're all men."

"We'll recheck right away. You know how tricky screen interpretation can be sometimes." Time Ops' tone was quietly apologetic, which was somehow more disturbing to

Derron than a chewing-out would have been. It meant that his position here was not considered so vital that Operations would bend every effort to make things go more smoothly for him.

The soldiers, after finishing their morning meal and emptying Derron's brandy flask, had for the most part settled down to serious loafing. Rudd, Vincento's coachman, was leading his load-beasts forth in search of grass. Following the animals through the gate, Derron located Vincento, sitting peacefully alone and apart with his writing materials. Well and good.

Remembering his imaginary load-beast and sulky, Derron put on an exasperated expression and strolled along the road toward the ruined bridge, scanning the fields in all directions as if in search of his missing property.

At the bridge-stump were the two friars, gray cowls thrown back from their unremarkable heads. Judging by their gestures and a word or two that floated Derron's way, they were talking of ways in which the bridge might someday be rebuilt. Derron knew that within a year or two there would indeed be new arches of stone spanning the river here. And those arches would still be standing solidly more than three hundred years later, when a young post-graduate history student would come striding over them on a hiking tour, the girl he loved striding just as eagerly beside him. Both of them would be enthusiastic about seeing for the first time the ancient town and the famed cathedral of Oibbog. . . . The river would look much different then, gentler, of course, and there would be more trees along its banks. While the stones of the ancient Empire road would still look much the same . . .

"May the Holy One give you a good day, esteemed sir!" It was the stouter of the two friars whose voice broke in upon Derron's reverie.

The interruption was welcome. "Good day to you also, reverend Brothers. Does the river still rise?"

The thinner friar had a loving face. In hands that seemed all bone and tendon, he was weighing a small chunk of masonry, as if he meant to start this minute to rebuild the bridge. "The river falls now, sir. How does the course of your life go, up or down?"

The falsehood about beast and buggy seemed dreary and unnecessary. "That can hardly be an easy question for any man to answer."

Derron was spared any further probing for the moment, as the attention of both friars had been distracted. Seven or eight of the local peasantry had materialized out of mud and distance and were plodding their barefoot way along the drying bank of the torrent toward the bridge-stump. One man walking in front of the others proudly swung a string of large and silvery fish, fresh enough to be still twitching and twisting.

A few paces away from the edge of the pavement, the peasants halted. Together they bowed rather perfunctorily in Derron's direction; he was not dressed finely enough to overawe anyone and he was obviously not the person the peasants had come to see.

The man who carried the fish began talking to the friars, in a low tone at first but raising his voice as the others began almost at once to interrupt him. In a few moments they were all squabbling over who had the right to speak first and whose was the right of disposal of the fish. They had come to strike a bargain. Would the holy brothers accept the biggest and freshest of this fine catch ("From me!" "No, from *me*, Holy Brother, it was my fishline!") and in return say some potent prayers for the giver's crops?

Derron turned away from what promised to become a nasty quarrel among the peasants, to see that Vincento was still sitting alone. And it was then that the full sunlit view of the Cathedral of Oibbog caught him almost by surprise.

The narrowed tip of the central spire held its gilded symbolic wedge two hundred and sixty feet above the flattened hilltop. The stones of tower and wall, of arch and flying buttress, were rich clear gray, almost shining in the morning light. Inside, he knew, the stained-glass windows along the eastern wall would be like living flame. If fragile glass and spire had risen from the dust, then surely she too must be alive, not only alive but somewhere near where he might reach her. At the moment the resurrected reality before him held more conviction than any rein of logic. At any second now, her voice might call to him, he might be able to reach out and touch . . .

There was a splash nearby. The stout friar was wearing a caricature-expression of anger, disappointment, and surprise, while the thinner one stood with a hand stretched out over the water. A big fish now jumped and splashed again; one of the slippery catch had evidently escaped.

. . . touch her warm and living skin. Now even a detail that he had somehow forgotten, the way her hair moved sometimes in the wind, came back to him with the visual clarity of something seen only a minute ago.

Derron's feet took him away from the bridge-stump and back along the road. He noted dutifully with half his mind that Vincento still sat alone in the sun. But Derron did not go back to the monastery. The hill raised the mighty cathedral before him, and he began steadily to climb.

Brother Jovann kept looking sadly at the peasants, even as he seemed to address his words to the splasher in the water. "Brother Fish, I have set you at liberty not because we do not need food, but so you may be able to praise God, who sends all blessings—the fish to the angler and freedom to the fish." Sorrowfully, Jovann shook his head at the peasants. "We men so often forget to give thanks when they are due, so often we spend our energy instead in trying to get ahead of one another!"

The fishes splashed, and leaped, and splashed again. It was as if the pain of the hook, or the time spent gilling air—or something else—had driven it quite mad.

Jovann looked down with new distress upon this watery uproar. "Be still now, Brother Fish! Enough! Live in the water, not the painful air. Give praise and thanks as a fish may naturally do!"

The splashing stopped. The last ripples and foam were swept away downstream.

Silence hung in the air. Every peasant's hands were raised in the wedge-sign, and they darted their eyes at one another as if they would have liked to take to their heels in flight, but did not dare. Brother Saile was gaping as blankly as any of the fish, while he swung his eyes from Jovann to the river and back again.

Jovann beckoned Saile away and said to him, "I am going apart for an hour, to pray to the Holy One to cleanse me of anger and pride. And also for these poor men's crops. Do you likewise." And Saile was left still staring, as Jovann walked slowly away alone, on up the road toward the monastery's gate.

As Derron climbed the steps that switchbacked up the face of the cathedral hill, the irrational sense of his love's presence faded, leaving him with only the bitter certainty of her permanent loss. It crossed his mind that at this moment in time her genes were scattered in the chromosomes of some two thousand ancestors. That was as close as he could come to her today, the closest he would ever be able to come. He knew that a solid palisade of paradox-loops would forever bar him from revisiting the days of her life, what he thought of as the time of his own youth.

The truth was that he had never forgiven her for dying, for being helplessly killed with all the other millions, for her crime of emptying his world. Maybe forgiving her was what he had come back to Oibbog to try to do. So, he told himself, do it. Do whatever is necessary to end it now, today. Get it all over with somehow, out of your system once and for all, so that you can be some good to yourself and to someone else again.

By now the roof of the monastery had fallen below the level of his climbing feet. When he looked back he saw the valley spreading out, flood-ravaged now and wilder in its beauty than he remembered it, but still essentially the same. At a turn on the stairs he passed a sapling and with a pang of realization he knew that in three hundred years this slender stem would be a gnarled and mighty trunk, with heavy branches to shade out the summer sun. And beside it he would stand with her, looking out over the valley, the two of them choosing a hill for themselves—that hill there, oh God, though no trees grew on it now!—where one day they intended to build their home and raise the pair of kids they meant to have.

He kept right on climbing. He felt that if he stopped here now he might never go on, and going on was necessary. Now at last his eyes rose above the level of the paved space before the main entrance of the cathedral. His memory recognized the very pattern of the paving stones here, where her feet and his would one day stand. If he stood here now, looking straight ahead at remembered hedges and statues, his vision bounded by the gray stone of the cathedral's front—why, for all that he could see or hear, holiday and youth and love might still be true, war and grief no more than bad dreams passing.

The twigs of the hedges were green again, with rain and late spring sunshine. But her voice was not to be heard here, nor would he ever again feel her touch, though he

were to stand here till he fell. And for a moment he
thought he might be going to fall, or to kneel and pray, or
to cry aloud, because the knowledge of her passing from
him was almost too much—but then, at long, long last,
that knowledge could be accepted.

The process of acceptance was not over in an instant,
but once it had fairly begun he knew he was not going to
collapse. His eyes were none too clear, but he was not
going to weep. He was just going to stand here and go on
living.

No, he was not finished yet. To complete the process of
acceptance and release he had still to go into the building,
where he had spent a morning helping her photograph the
stained glass. He remembered wishing aloud at that time
that the supposed Author of the universe would come out
of hiding and make an appearance in this, supposedly His
temple; because the young historian had a few sharp questions that he wanted to ask. Questions having to do with
the unnecessary amount of injustice in the world.

The great door was just as solidly hung as Derron remembered it. He wondered briefly if a wooden door in
steady use might last three hundred years. No matter. He
tugged it open, hearing the booming reverberation of the
broken closure come back with repetitions from the building's cavernous interior. Just then it crossed Derron's mind
that his traveler's staff with all its weaponry was resting
back in his monastery cell. But that was no matter; immediate violence from the berserker was not a danger.

He went in and paced down the center of the nave,
which was only about thirty feet wide between the rows of
columns that divided it from the side aisles, but enormous
in its other dimensions—three hundred feet long, the
keystones of its arches a hundred feet above the floor.
There seemed room in here for God and berserker both to
hide, with plenty of corners left to conceal some deserter

or pregnant waif whose lifeline might be showing up to confuse Operations.

Along the eastern wall the stained-glass windows flamed. Centuries of candle smoke had not yet darkened the high arches. Most of the cathedral had been built during the last generation; in fact, construction had not been quite completed when this latest war had resulted in the workmen being ordered or frightened off the job. Much scaffolding still surrounded columns and clung to walls, here and there festooned with the workmen's abandoned ropes and cables, which were as steady in the motionless air as if carved from stone themselves. A few abandoned tools were very slowly gathering dust where they had been set down.

Whether because of the combatants' reverence or superstitious fear, or only through chance, war had not trampled here. Even the stained glass was all intact, splintered only by the sun coming in to fire the mild gloom with richness. The wide steps that led to side chapels, and most of the paving of the nave, were no more than a century old, still flat and practically unworn; three centuries and more of random footsteps would be required to shape them into standard distribution curves.

As Derron approached the center of the building, where nave and transepts intersected, a movement caught the corner of his eye. One of the friars, hood worn over his head here in God's house, was approaching him down a side aisle.

Derron stopped, nodding politely. "Reverend Brother." And then it struck him as odd that one of the men he had left down at the bridge should have hurried here ahead of him. Peering closely, he saw that the face beneath the cowl was not quite a face. And the hands reaching out to grab him as the figure shot forward were dummy flesh, split open now to show the steel claws.

*   *   *

The leaner of the friars had come dragging along, head bowed, up the road from the bridge. He passed the monastery's gateway, and Vincento was just thinking with some relief that the man was going right on by him, when at the last moment the friar appeared to become aware of Vincento and, after a little startled pause, changed course and came toward him.

He stopped a couple of paces away, smiling now, a gentle and bedraggled figure. "God will reward you, Vincent, for providing my companions and me with food."

"God knows I have some need of His favor, Brother," Vincento answered shortly. He supposed the mendicant had learned his given name from Rudd or Will. Curiously, he did not feel offended by the familiar form of address; the dusty beggar before him seemed, like an infant, beneath any question of status.

But Vincento remained wary. It was just possible that this friar was one of the Defenders' agents.

The friar was looking at the papers spread out before Vincento as he might have regarded some friend's unbandaged wound. "Vincent, why do you waste your mind and soul in all these struggles and disputes? Their outcome does not matter, really. But one thing matters, and that is the love of God."

The mad innocent sincerity of these words all but wiped away Vincento's suspicions and could provoke him to nothing stronger than a smile. "It seems you have taken the trouble to learn something of my affairs. But, reverend Brother, what do you really understand of my disputes and why I have them?"

The friar drew back with a little quiver of distaste. "I do not understand them. I do not wish to; it is not my way."

"Then, Brother, pardon me, but it seems to me you should not lecture on what you do not understand, nor stand here disputing with me as to why I have disputes."

The friar accepted the rebuke so meekly that Vincento felt a momentary pang of something like regret for having spoken it. And with that the dispute between them, if one could really call it that, was over, Vincento having scored his point with the ease of an armored knight knocking down a child.

The friar did not turn away before he had raised his hands in blessing and murmured a few words that were not addressed to Vincento. Then he departed at once, walking slowly on along the road—once hesitating as if on the point of turning back, then going on. It crossed Vincento's mind that he had once again won an argument and perhaps lost something else—though what it was one lost on these occasions he could not exactly say. He almost called after the man, feeling an impulse to try to reach across the gap between then. But he did not call. Really, he thought, we have nothing to say to each other.

Now that he had been distracted from the humiliating task of writing his recantation, he did not want to take it up again. And so Vincento summoned Will, gave him the escritoire and papers to take in charge, and then turned his own steps restlessly upward in the fine sunlight.

Thinking it over now, he decided that the meeting supposedly arranged in the cathedral was most probably a snare of the Defenders—or more likely, of some of Vincento's enemies, religious or laymen, who would be eager to trick him into some compromising utterance or behavior on the eve of his trial. Very well, let them try. He would see through the scheme, whatever it was, before they had gotten very far with it. He might be able to turn the tables on them completely. Vincent might fear men who overmatched him in power, but he knew full well that none could overmatch him in intelligence.

He was patient with his old legs, resting them for a single breath after every two or three steps, and so they served him well enough on the climb. After a longer pause for rest at the top of the stairs, he entered at the cathedral's main door and tugged it firmly closed behind him. He devoutly hoped that no one was going to meet him simply to offer sympathy. A sympathizer was at best a secret gloater, having always at least some implied claim to be the equal—more like the superior!—of the one he supposedly was trying to console. Pah!

Vincento strolled through the nave, a stone-sealed space too vast to give the least sense of confinement. To his right and left, the vault-supporting columns towered in their parallel rows. Distance diminished the apparent space between each column and the next, until at fifty paces ahead of him each row became opaque as a wall. No matter where a man stood inside this unpartitioned space, half of it would always be blocked from his view—more than half, if one counted the areas of the transept arms and the chapels.

When he reached the appointed meeting place, the crossways of nave and transepts, Vincento could look directly up nearly two hundred feet into the shadowed interior of the temple's mighty central spire. There were workmen's platforms even there, reached by ladders mounting from the clerestory level, which in turn must be accessible by some stair coiling up within the wall from the level of the floor Vincento stood upon.

In this temple, built in the grand old style, there were no chandeliers, and no breezes to swing them if they had existed. If in Vincento's youth this had been his parish house of worship, he would have had to begin to work out the laws of pendulums somewhere else, and not during a drowsy Sabbath sermon.

A single cable of great length descended thinly from the uttermost dark interior of the spire. Vincento's eye followed this cable down, to discover that there was a pendulum here after all, at least in potential. For bob, there hung on the end of the long cable a ball of metal that would be as heavy as a man. This weight was pulled to one side, held by the merest loop of cord to one of the four thick columns that stood at the corners of the nave-transept intersection.

Looking up and down, up and down again, tended to make an old man dizzy. Vincento rubbed his neck. But there was an offense to logic here that was beyond his power to ignore. What use could the builders have had for such a patriarch of pendulums?

It *could*, he supposed, be something that they swung when hard stone and mortar had to be demolished—but that was hardly a satisfactory explanation. And if it was only a plumb line, why so weighty? A few ounces of lead would serve that purpose just as well.

Whatever they had intended or used it for, it *was* a pendulum. The restraining tether of cord, with its single knot, looked insubstantial. Vincento thrummed the taut little cord with his finger, and the long, lone cable gently whipped and swayed. The massive weight made little bobbing motions, dipping like a ship at anchor.

The oscillations quickly died away, the stillness of the cathedral soon regained ascendancy. Once more cord and cable and bob were as steady as the stone columns in the still gray air. The pendulum-ship was drydocked.

Set sail, then! On impulse Vincento tugged once at the end of the restraining cord. And with startling ease the knot dissolved.

Starting from rest, the weight for a moment seemed reluctant to move at all. And even after it had undeniably begun its first swing, still it moved so slowly that Vincento's eye went involuntarily racing once more up into the shadows of the spire, to see how it was possible that mere length of cord should so delay things.

A man might have counted four without haste before the weight for the first time reached the center, the low point, of its swing. Almost touching the floor, it passed that center in a smooth fast rush and immediately began to slow again, so that it needed four more counts to climb the gentle gradient of the far half of its arc. Then the weight paused for an unmeasurable instant, not quite touching the column at the opposite corner of the crossways, before it crept into its returning motion.

Majestically the bob went back and forth, holding its cable taut, describing a perfect arc segment about ten yards in length. Vincento's eye could find no diminution in the amplitude of the first half-dozen swings. He supposed that a weight so heavy and so freely suspended as this might continue to oscillate for many hours or even for days.

Wait, though. Here was something. Vincento squinted at the pendulum through one swing. Then, leaning against the column it had been tethered to, and holding his head motionless, he watched the pendulum's swing end-on for another half-dozen cycles.

What was it he had come in here for? Oh, yes, someone was perhaps going to meet him.

But this pendulum. He frowned at it, shook his head and watched some more. Then he started to look around him. He was going to have to make sure of something he thought he saw.

Some workmen's sawhorses were standing not far away. He dragged a pair of these to where he wanted them, so that the plank he now took up and set across them lay beneath the end of the pendulum's arc and perpendicular to that arc's direction. On the bottom of the swinging weight he had noticed a projection like a small spike: whatever it had been meant for, it would serve Vincento's present purpose well. He laid a second plank atop the first, and slightly readjusted the position of his whole structure, in careful increments. Now on each swing the spike passed within an inch of the topmost board.

He would make marks upon the board . . . but no, he could do better. Somewhere in here he had seen sand. Yes, piled in a mixing trough, there by the entrance to the first side chapel. The sand was satisfactorily damp from the long spell of wet weather; he brought handfuls of it and dumped them on his upper board. Along several feet of the board's length he patted and built the sand into a tiny wall, an inch or two high and just thick enough to stand. Then, in an interval between swings, he slid that upper board just slightly forward, taking his sand wall into the edge of the pendulum's arc.

A neatly designed experiment, he thought with satisfaction. On its first return, the moving spike notched his little sand fence delicately, tumbling a tiny clot of grains down the minute slope. Then the weight pulled its taut cable away again, taking another slow nibble of eternity.

Vincento held his eyes from blinking as he watched the pendulum's return. Holding his breath too, he could now hear for the first time the faint ghostly hissing of the swing.

The spike as it moved back to the wall of sand made a new notch, though one contiguous with the first. Then the weight once more departed, in a movement huge and regular enough to be the cathedral's stately pulse.

And sixteen seconds later the third notch was new again, by the same margin and in the same direction as the second. In three vibrations the plane of the pendulum had shifted its extremity sideways by half a finger-width. His eyes had not deceived him earlier; that plane was slowly and regularly creeping clockwise.

Might this effect be due to some slow untwisting of the cable? Then it should soon reverse itself, Vincento thought, or at least vary in amplitude. Again he stared up into the high shadows, oblivious of his aching neck.

If he could, he would someday, somewhere, hang another pendulum like this one and study it at leisure. Yes, if he could. Even supposing that his health held out and that he was spared prison, it would be difficult. Enclosed towers of this height were anything but common. In another big temple or at some university, perhaps—but he had no intention of stooping to collaboration.

. . . Suppose now that the puzzling sideways progression was *not* due to the cable's unwinding. He thought he could feel that it was not, in somewhat the same way as, after study, he had come to feel certain of the stability of the sun. This clockwise creeping had something too elemental about it for him to be able to credit a trivial cause.

Already the width of two fingers had been nibbled from the top of his little parapet of sand.

He wondered how the cable was fastened at the top. Younger legs than his would be required to find that out, and Vincento departed to obtain them. Several times in his passage down the nave he turned, frowning back at the ceaseless pendulum as he might have stared at an unexpected star.

Of it all, Derron had seen only an upper segment of the moving cable. He saw even that much with only one eye, for his face was being held with steady force against the rough planking of the high platform to which he had been carried, helpless as a kicking infant in the grip of the berserker. Inhumanly motionless, it crouched over him now, one chill hand gripping his neck and holding part of his coat gaglike in his mouth, the other hand twisting one of his arms just to the point of pain.

Obviously the machine had no intention of killing or crippling him, not here. Still, his captivity seemed less like a period of time than a segment of eternity, measured out by the meaningless regularity of the swinging cable. Having him prisoner, the berserker was content to wait, which meant he had already failed. He had not had time even to communicate his situation to Operations: the berserker had at once known his pectoral wedge for what it was; it had ripped the wooden carving from his neck and cracked it like a thin-shelled nut, squeezing the meat of metal and components into trash between its fingers.

Perhaps it thought that he could see nothing from the position in which it held him. That was almost true. From the tail of one eye he could just descry that metronomic cable, its arc narrow at this height, but its slow movement speaking of its enormous length.

At that the cathedral door far below boomed shut for the second time since he had been captured. And only then did eternity begin to come to an end; the berserker let him go.

Slowly and painfully he raised his half-numbed body from the wood. Rubbing the cheek that had been ground against the platform and the arm that had been twisted, he turned to face his enemy. Under the monk's cowl he saw a pattern of seamed metal that looked as if it might be able to open and slide and reshape itself. He knew that he was facing what was probably the most complex and compact machine that the berserkers had ever built. Inside that steel skull, could there be plastic skin that could evert to become the convincing mask of a human face? There was no way to tell that much, let alone guess what identity it might be able to wear.

"Colonel Odegard," it said, in a voice machine-tailored to neutrality.

Taken somewhat by surprise, he waited to hear more, while the thing facing him on the high platform squatted on its heels, arms hanging limp. The hands were as ambiguous as the face; they were not human now, but there was no saying what they might be able to become.

The rest of the body was hidden under the shapeless robe, which had probably once been Amling's.

"Colonel Odegard, do you fear the passage from life to not-life?"

He didn't know what he had expected to hear, but hardly that. "And if I do, what difference does it make?"

"Yes," said the berserker in its flat voice. "What is programmed goes on, regardless of any passage."

Before he could try to make any sense out of that, the machine jumped precisely forward and grabbed him again. He struggled, which of course made no difference. It tore strips from his coat, ripping the tough cloth with precise and even sounds. With the strips it gagged him again and tied him hand and foot—tightly, but not so tightly that he felt no hope of ever working free. It was not going to blunder into being responsible for a death here in the safety zone.

After it had bound him, the machine paused for a moment, moving its cowled head like a listening man, searching the area with senses far beyond the human. And then it was gone down the ladder in utter silence, moving less like a man than like a giant cat or ape.

He could only strain desperately to get free, the gag choking back his curses.

A second group of peasants, from some village higher in the hills, had come along the road to the cathedral. It was Brother Saile they met first; when they learned that he was not the saint and miracle worker of whom the whole countryside was talking, a brief glow of hope died from their faces, leaving only bitter anxiety.

"Tell me, what is it you wish to see Brother Jovann about?" Saile inquired magisterially, clasping his hands with dignity across his belly.

They clamored piteously, all at once, until he had to

speak sharply to get them to talk one at a time and make
sense. Then he heard that, for several days past, a great
wolf had been terrorizing their little village. The mon-
strous beast had killed cattle and even—they swore it!
—uprooted crops. The peasants were all talking at once
again, and Saile was not sure if they said a child had been
devoured, or if a herd boy had fallen and broken his arm,
trying to get away from the wolf. In any case, the villagers
were desperate. Men scarcely dared to work their fields.
They were isolated, and very poor, with no powerful
patron to give them aid of any kind, save only the Holy
One Himself! And now the saintly Jovann, who must and
would do *something!* They were utterly desperate!

Brother Saile nodded. In his manner there showed sympathy mixed with reluctance. "And you say your village is
several miles distant? In the hills, yes. Well—we shall see.
I will do my best for you. Come with me and I will put
your case before good Brother Jovann."

With a puzzled Will now walking beside him, Vincento
entered the cathedral once more and made the best speed
that he could down the nave. Back at the monastery, Rudd
had chosen this time to bother him with warnings and
complaints about the scarcity of food for the beasts. And
when he had disentangled himself from that, his old legs
had rebelled against climbing the hill a second time, even
with Will's help. Now as Vincento hurried, wheezing for
breath, back to his still-swinging pendulum, more than an
hour had passed since he had first set the bob in motion.

For a few seconds he only stared in thoughtful silence at
what had happened since his departure. The tiny battle-
ment of sand had been demolished by continuous notches,
up to the point where the pendulum's turning plane had
left it behind altogether. That plane had by now inched
clockwise through ten or twelve degrees of arc.

"Will, you've helped me in the workship. Now this is another such case, where you must follow my orders precisely."

"Aye, master."

"First, keep in mind that you are not to stop the swinging of this cable here or disturb it in any way. Understood?"

"Aye."

"Good. Now I want you to climb; there seem to be ladders and platforms enough for you to go up all the way. I want to discover how this swinging cable is mounted, what holds it at the top. Look at it until you can make me a sketch, you have a fair hand at drawing."

"Aye, I understand, sir." Will craned his neck unhappily. "It's longish bit o' climbin', though."

"Yes, yes, a coin for you when you're down. Another when you've given me a good sketch. Take your time now, and use your eyes. And remember, do not disturb the cable's swing."

Derron had made only moderate progress toward getting the bonds loosened from his wrists when he heard clumsier feet than the berserker's climbing toward him. Between the ladder's uprights Will's honest face came into view, then predictably registered shock.

". . . Bandit!" Derron spat, when his hands had been cut free and he could rid himself of the gag. "Must've been hiding in here somewhere . . . forced me up here and tied me up."

"Robbed ye, hey?" Will was awed. "Just one of 'em?"

"Yes, just one. Uh . . . I didn't have any valuables with me, really. Took the wedge from around my neck."

"That's fearsome. One o' them lone rogues, hey?" Wondering and sympathetic, Will shook his head. "Likely he'd a' slit your throat, sir, but didn't want to do no real sacrilege. Think he might still be here about?"

"No, no, I'm sure he was running away. Long gone by this time."

Will went on shaking his head. "Well. You'd better liven up your limbs, sir, before you starts to climb down. I'm going on up, bit of a job to do for master."

"Job?"

"Aye." Will was already climbing again, seemingly meaning to go right on up into the spire.

Still on all fours, Derron peered down over the edge of the platform. Vincento's ginger-colored hair marked a toy figure more than a hundred feet below. Down there the mysteriously moving cable ended in a dot, a ball of some kind that was tracing back and forth with sedate regularity. Derron had seen a pendulum of this size and shape before, somewhere. It had been used as a demonstration of . . .

Derron's muscles locked, after a moment in which he had been near falling over the platform's edge. He had suddenly realized what Vincento was looking at, what Vincento doubtless had been studying for most of the time Derron had been held captive. On old Earth they had honored its earliest known inventor by naming it the Foucault pendulum.

"Honorable Vincento!"

Vincento looked around in surprise and annoyance to discover the young man, Alzay or Valzay or whatever his name was, hurrying toward Vincento in obvious agitation, having evidently just descended from the tiny coiled stair where Will had begun his climb.

Valzay came hurrying up as if bringing the most vital news, though when he arrived all he had to relate was some imbecilic story about a bandit. Valzay's eyes were looking sharply at the sawhorses and planks and the little wall of sand, even as he spouted pestiferous wordage that threatened to tangle Vincento's thoughts.

Vincento interrupted him. "Young man, I suggest you give your recital to the soldiers." Then he turned his back on the intruder. Now. If it was *not* the cable untwisting, and if it proved to be *not* some trick of the mounting above—then what? Certainly the bones of the cathedral were not creeping counterclockwise. But yet . . . His mind strained forward, sounding unknown depths. . . .

"I see, Messire Vincento, that you have already discovered my little surprise." Derron saw very clearly how the game was certain to go, how it perhaps had gone already. But he also saw one desperate gamble that was still open to him and he seized the chance.

"Your—little—surprise?" Vincento's voice became very deliberate. His brows knit as if presaging thunder, while he turned slowly back to face Derron. "Then it was you who sent that rascally friar to me in the night?"

The detail of the friar was confirmation, if any was needed, of what the berserker planned. "It was I who arranged this!" Derron gestured with proprietary pride at the pendulum. "I must confess, sir, that I have really been here for several days; at first in the company of some friends, who aided me in this construction."

It was a big lie that Derron was improvising, and one that would not stand investigation. But if it had the initial impact that he hoped it would, Vincento would never want to investigate.

As he told the silent, grim old man how he and his imaginary aides had installed the pendulum, Derron visualized the berserker here at work, catlike, monkeylike, devilish, arranging mounting and cable and weight in order that . . .

". . . you see before you, Messire Vincento, a firm proof of the rotation of the globe!"

There was a startled gleam in the old eyes, but no real surprise. Beyond a doubt the desperate gamble had been justified. Now, to see if it could be won. Vincento had become a waiting statue, mouth twisted, eyes unblinking.

Derron spoke on. "Of course, I have followed your example, distinguished sir, and that of several of our contemporaries, in protecting rightful claim to this discovery while still keeping it secret for my own advantage in further research. To this end I have sent to several distinguished persons, in several parts of the world, anagram messages which encode a description of this experiment.

"This to keep the secret yet awhile was, as I say, my plan. But when word reached me of your present—*difficulties*—I found I could not stand idly by."

Vincento had not yet moved. "A proof of our globe's rotation, you say." The tone was flat, suspended.

"Ah, forgive me! I had not thought an explanation in detail would be—um. You see, the plane of the pendulum does not rotate, it is our globe that rotates beneath it." Derron hesitated briefly—it was just occurring to Valzay that old Vincento had most likely become just a little slow, a trifle senile. Derron put on what he hoped looked like a faintly indulgent smile and spoke on, more slowly and distinctly. "At the poles of the world, such a device as this would trace daily a full circle of three hundred and sixty degrees. At the equator it would appear not to rotate at all." Speeding up gradually, he poured in merciless detail his three and a half centuries' advantage in accumulated knowledge. "Between these extremes, the rate of rotation is proportional to the latitude; here, it is about ten degrees per hour. And since we are in the northern hemisphere, the direction of apparent rotation is clockwise. . . ."

From high above, Will was shouting down to his master, "She be mounted free to turn any way, but there be nothing turning her!"

Vincento shouted up, "Come down!"

". . . bit more study if 'ee wants a sketch—"

"Come down!" The thick lips spat it out.

Derron kept the pressure on as best he could, switching the emphasis now to relentless generosity. "My only wish, of course, is to help you, sir. I have put aside thoughts of personal advantage to come to your rescue. In bygone days you have accomplished very substantial things, very substantial, and you must not now be cast aside. My lance is at your disposal; I will gladly repeat this demonstration of my discovery for the authorities in the Holy City, so that the entire world may witness—"

"Enough! I have no need of *help!*" Vincento made the last word an obscenity. "You will not—meddle—in—my—affairs. Not in the least degree!"

In his contempt and wrath the old man became a towering figure. Derron found himself physically retreating—even as he realized that he had won his gamble, that Vincento's pride was indeed as monumental as his genius.

The outburst of proud anger was short-lived. Derron ceased retreating and stood in silence as Vincento, shrinking once more under his burdens of age and weariness and fear, shot him a parting look of hate and turned away. Now Vincento would never use the Foucault proof, nor believe it, nor even investigate in that direction. He would force the whole thing from his mind if he could. The smallness and jealousy that were leading Vincento on to trial and humiliation existed not only in other men, but in himself.

Derron knew from history that at his trial Vincento would not only recant, he would go beyond what his judges asked or wanted of him and offer to write a new pamphlet, proving that the sun did after all fly in a circle around the world of men.

My only wish is to help you, sir. Vincento's shuffling figure dwindled at last to the end of the nave, and at last the door boomed shut behind him. Exhausted, Derron sagged against a column, hearing now in the silence the pendulum's unperturbed repeated hiss. Will came scrambling down the stair to scowl uncomprehendingly at him and then hurry on after his master.

And now even Vincento's tragedy could be forgotten for the moment. Real victory and real hope were powerful stimulants. They gave Derron energy enough to hurry out of the cathedral by a side door and go skipping down a steep stair that led directly to the monastery. If the berserker had not also smashed the backup communication hidden in his staff, he could transmit the joy of victory at once to all the Modern world.

The enemy had not bothered with anything in his cell. As he hurried toward it along the vaulted passage, an emergency summons from Operations began to throb in the bone behind his ear.

Brother Saile was puffing, though he had certainly been making no effort to hurry. The narrow cattle path the friars were following went mostly up and down hill, winding its way through scrubby bushes and thin woods. Saile was actually hanging back, and trying, with almost every labored breath, to discourage Brother Jovann from going on.

"I thought—to have said a few prayers in the village—would have been sufficient. These peasants, as you know—are often foolish. They may have—greatly exaggerated—the depredations of this—supposed wolf."

"Then my own peasant foolishness is not likely to cause any harm," said Jovann, leading on implacably. They were miles from the cathedral now, deep in the wolf's supposed domain. Their peasant supplicants and guides had turned back through fear a quarter of a mile earlier.

"I spoke too harshly of them. May the Holy One forgive me." Saile wheezed to the top of a hill and gathered breath for readier speech on the descent. "Now, if this one beast has really caused in a few days all the death and damage attributed to it, or even half so much, it would be utter folly for us to approach it, unarmed as we are. It is not that I doubt for an instant the inscrutable wisdom of Providence that can cause a fish to leap for joy after you have released it, nor do I doubt the story that is told of the gentle little birds listening to your preaching. But a wolf, and especially such a wolf as this, is quite another . . ."

Brother Jovann did not appear to be listening very closely. He had paused briefly to follow with his eyes a train of scavenger insects, which crossed the path and vanished into the brush. Then he went on, more slowly, until a similar file appeared a little farther along the trail. There Brother Jovann turned aside and walked noisily into the brush, leading his companion toward the spot where it seemed the two lines of insects must intersect.

Staff in hand, Derron made the best cross-country time he could, running fifty steps and walking fifty.

"Odegard!" Time Ops had cried out. "There's another lifeline just as vital as Vincento's right there with you. Or he was with you. Now he and one of the others have moved out a couple of miles; they're about to leave the safety zone. You've got to get there and protect him somehow. The berserker will have him cold if it's out there waiting!"

And of course it would be out there, in ambush or pursuit. The attack on Vincento had been in deadly earnest, as the first punch in any good one-two should be. But it was the second punch that was really expected to get through and do the damage. And humanity had been left wide open for this one.

Running fifty steps, walking fifty, Derron steadily covered ground along the bearing Operations had given him. He asked, "Just who am I looking for?"

And when they told him, he thought he should have guessed the name, should have been alerted by his first look into that loving face.

In the midst of the thicket there had been havoc. It had happened days ago, for the tree branches that had been broken were now quite dead. And though the insects were still busy amid the wreckage of bone and gray fur on the ground, there was no longer much for them to scavenge.

"This was a very big wolf," said Brother Jovann thoughtfully, bending to pick up a piece of jawbone. The bone had been shattered by some violent blow, but this fragment still contained teeth of impressive size.

"Very big, certainly," agreed Brother Saile, though he knew little about wolves and had no wish to learn any more. He kept looking about him nervously. The sun was slanting into late afternoon, and to Saile the forest seemed ominously still.

Jovann was musing aloud. "Now, what manner of creature can it be that deals thus with a big male wolf? Even as I in my greed have sometimes dealt with the bones of a little roast fowl . . . but no, these bones have not been gnawed for nourishment. Only broken, and broken again, as if by some creature more wantonly savage than any wolf."

The name of Brother Jovann symbolized gentleness and love to Modern historians as well as laymen, to skeptics as well as the orthodox temple-members who venerated him as a saint. Like Vincento, St. Jovann had become a towering folk figure, only half-understood.

"We're just this hour catching on to Jovann's practical importance," said Time Ops' voice in Derron's head, as

Derron ran. "With Vincento stabilized, and all our observers concentrated on the area you're in, we're getting a better look at it than ever before. Historically, Jovann's lifeline goes on about fifteen years from your point, and all along the way it radiates support to other lines. What has been described as 'good-turn-a-day stuff.' Then these other lines tend to radiate life support in turn, and the process propagates on up through history. Our best judgment now is that the disarmament treaty three hundred years after Jovann's death will fall through, and that an international nuclear war will wipe out our civilization in pre-Modern times, if St. Jovann is terminated at your point."

When Time Ops paused, a girl's voice came in briskly. "A new report for Colonel Odegard."

Walking again, Derron asked, "Lisa?"

She hesitated for just an instant, then continued, business first. "Colonel, the lifeline that was described to you earlier as having an embryonic appearance is moving out of the safety zone after the other two. It seems to be traveling at a high rate of speed, faster than a man or a load-beast can run. We can give no explanation of this. Also, you're to bear five degrees left."

"Understand." Derron turned five degrees left, as near as he could judge. He was getting out of the lowlands now, and there was a little less mud to impede his progress. "Lisa?"

"Derron, they let me come on because I said I'd tend strictly to business."

"Understand. You do that." He judged he had walked fifty steps and began to run once more, his breath immediately turning into gasps. "I just want to say—I wish—you were carrying my baby."

There was a small, completely feminine sound. But when Lisa's voice came back on intelligibly, it was cool again, with more bearing corrections to be given.

*   *   *

From the corner of his eye Brother Saile caught the distant moving of something running toward them through the trees and brush. He turned, squinting under the afternoon sun, and with surprise at his own relative calm he saw that their search for the wolf had come to an end. Wolf? The thing approaching should perhaps be called monster or demon instead, but he could not doubt it was the creature that had spread terror among the peasants, come now to find the men who dared to search for it.

Poisonous-looking as a silver wasp, the man-sized creature was still a hundred yards away, running through the scrub forest silent, catlike, four-legged. Brother Saile realized that he should now attempt to lay down his life for his friend, he should shove Brother Jovann back and rush forward himself to distract the thing. And something in Brother Saile wanted to achieve such heroism, but his belly and feet had now turned to lead, leaving him immobile as a statue. He tried to shout a warning, but even his throat was paralyzed by fear. At last he did manage to seize Brother Jovann by the arm and point.

"Ah," said Jovann, coming out of a reverie and turning to look. A score of paces away, the monster was slowing to a halt, crouching on its four slender legs, looking from one friar to the other as if to decide which of them it wanted. Peasants glimpsing the creature might call it wolf. Shreds of gray fabric festooned it here and there, as if it had been clothed and then had, beastlike, torn itself out of the garment. Naked and hairless and sexless, terrible and beautiful at once, it flowed like quicksilver as it took two rapid strides closer to the men. Then it settled again into a crouching, silent statue.

"In God's n-name, come away!" Brother Saile whispered, his jaws shivering. "It is no natural beast. Come away, Brother Jovann!"

But Jovann only raised his hands and signed the horror with the wedge; he seemed to be blessing it rather than exorcising.

"Brother Wolf," he said lovingly, "you do indeed look unlike any beast that I have ever seen before, and I know not from what worldly parentage you may have sprung. But there is in you the spirit of life; therefore never forget that our Father above has created you, as He has created all other creatures, so we are all children of the one Father."

The wolf darted forward and stopped, stepped and stopped, inched up and stopped again, in a fading oscillation. In its open mouth Saile thought he saw fangs not only long and sharp, but actually blurring with vicious motion like the teeth of some incredible saw. At last there came forth a sound, and Saile was reminded simultaneously of ringing sword blades and of human agony.

Jovann dropped to one knee, facing the crouching monster more on a level. He spread his arms as if willing an embrace. The thing bounded in a blur of speed toward him, then stopped as if a leash had caught it. It was still six or eight paces from the kneeling man. Again it uttered a sound; Saile, half-fainting, seemed to hear the creak of the torture rack and the cry of the victim rise together.

Jovann's voice had nothing in it of fear, but only blended sternness with its love.

"Brother Wolf, you have killed and pillaged like a wanton criminal, and for that you deserve punishment! But accept instead the forgiveness of all the men you have wronged. Come now, here is my hand. In the name of the Holy One, come to me, and pledge that from this day on you will live at peace with men. Come!"

Derron, approaching at a staggering, exhausted run, first heard a murmur of speech, and then saw the figure of

Brother Saile standing motionless, looking off to one side at something concealed from Derron by a thicket. Derron lurched to a halt, raising his staff but not yet aiming it. He knew now that Saile was not the berserker. What Operations had reported about the embryo-like lifeline had fitted in at last in Derron's mind with something the berserker had said to him in the cathedral, fitted in to make a wondrous kind of sense. Three steps sideways brought Derron to where he could see what Saile was gaping at.

He had come in time to see the berserker-wolf take the last hesitant step in its advance. To see it raise one metal paw—and with its steel claw-fingers gently touch the kneeling friar's extended hand.

"So, my guess was right; it had become a living thing," said Derron. His head was resting in Lisa's lap, and he could if he chose look up past her face at the buried park's real tree tops and artificial sun. "And, as such, susceptible to St. Jovann's domination. To his love . . . I guess there's no other way to put it."

Lisa, stroking his forehead, raised her eyebrows questioningly.

Derron put on a defensive frown. "Oh, there are rational explanations. The most complex and compact machine the berserkers ever built, driven up through twenty thousand years of evolutionary gradient from their staging area—something like life was bound to happen to it. Or so we say now. And Jovann and some other men have had amazing power over living things; that's fairly well documented, even if we rationalists can't understand it."

"I looked up the story about St. Jovann and the wolf," said Lisa, still stroking his brow. "It says that, after he tamed it, the animal lived out its days like a pet dog in the village."

"That would refer to the original wolf. . . . I guess the

little change in history we had wasn't enough to change the legend. I suppose it was the berserker's plan all along to kill the original animal and take its place during the taming episode. Killing Jovann then might make people think he had been a fraud all his life. But tearing the original wolf into bits was an irrational, lifelike thing to do—if we'd known about that sooner, we might have guessed what'd happened to our enemy. There were other little clues along the way—things it did for no reason that would be valid for a machine. And I really should have guessed in the cathedral, when it started babbling to me about passages between life and not-life. Anyway, Operations isn't as trusting as Jovann and his biographers. We've got the thing in a cage in present-time while the scientists try to decide what to . . ."

Derron had to pause there, to accommodate a young lady who was bending over him with the apparent intention of being kissed.

". . . Did I mention how nice some of that country looked around there?" he went on, a little later. "Of course, the big hill is reserved for the rebuilding of the cathedral. But I thought you and I might drop into a Homestead Office some time soon, you know, before the postwar rush starts, and put our names down for one of those other hilltops. . . ."

And Derron had to pause again.

Not science nor music nor any other art encompasses the full measure of life's refusal to succumb. The pattern is as deep as the blind growth of cells, as high as the loftiest intellect—and broader than we can see as yet.

SMASHER

CLAUS SLOVENSKO WAS COMING TO THE CONCLUSION THAT THE battle in nearby space was going to be invisible to anyone on the planet Waterfall—assuming that there was really going to be a battle at all.

Claus stood alone atop a forty-meter dune, studying a night sky that flamed with the stars of the alien Busog cluster, mostly blue-white giants which were ordinarily a sight worth watching in themselves. Against that background, the greatest energies released by interstellar warships could, he supposed, be missed as a barely visible twinkling. Unless, of course, the fighting should come very close indeed.

In the direction he was facing, an ocean made invisible by night stretched from near the foot of the barren dune to a horizon marked only by the cessation of the stars. Claus turned now to scan once more the sky in the other direction. That way, toward planetary north, the starry profusion went on and on. In the northeast a silvery half-moon, some antique stage designer's concept of what Earth's own moon should be, hung low behind thin clouds. Below those clouds extended an entire continent of lifeless sand and rock. The land masses of Waterfall were bound in a silence that Earth ears found uncanny, stillness marred only by the wind, by murmurings of sterile streams, and by occasional deep rumblings in the rock itself.

Claus continued turning slowly, till he faced south again. Below him the night sea lapped with lulling false familiarity. He sniffed the air, and shrugged, and gave up squinting at the stars, and began to feel his way, one cautious

foot after another, down the shifting slope of the dune's
flank. A small complex of buildings, labs and living quarters bunched as if for companionship, the only human
habitation on the world of Waterfall, lay a hundred meters
before him and below. Tonight as usual the windows were
all cheerfully alight. Ino Vacroux had decided, and none
of the other three people on the planet had seen any reason
to dispute him, that any attempt at blackout would be
pointless. If a berserker force was going to descend on
Waterfall, the chance of four defenseless humans avoiding
discovery by the unliving killers would be nil.

Just beyond the foot of the dune, Claus passed through
a gate in the high fence of fused rock designed to keep out
drifting sand—with no land vegetation of any kind to hold
the dunes in place, they tended sometimes to get pushy.

A few steps past the fence, he opened the lockless door
of the main entrance to the comfortable living quarters.
The large common room just inside was cluttered with
casual furniture, books, amateur art, and small and middle-
sized aquariums. The three other people who completed
the population of the planet were all in this room at the
moment, and all looked up to see if Claus brought news.

Jenny Surya, his wife, was seated at the small computer
terminal in the far corner, wearing shorts and sweater,
dark hair tied up somewhat carelessly, long elegant legs
crossed. She was frowning as she looked up, but abstract-
edly, as if the worst news Claus might be bringing them
would be of some potential distraction from their work.

Closer to Claus, in a big chair pulled up to the big
communicator cabinet, slouched Ino Vacroux, senior scientist of the base. Claus surmised that Ino had been a
magnificent physical specimen a few decades ago, before
being nearly killed in a berserker attack upon another
planet. The medics had restored function but not fineness
to his body. The gnarled, hairy thighs below his shorts

were not much thicker than a child's; his ravaged torso was draped now in a flamboyant shirt. In a chair near him sat Glenna Reyes, his wife, in her usual work garb of clean white coveralls. She was just a little younger than Vacroux, but wore the years with considerably more ease.

"Nothing to see," Claus informed them all, with a loose wave meant to describe the lack of visible action in the sky.

"Or to hear, either," Vacroux grated. His face was grim as he nodded toward the communicator. The screens of the device sparkled, and its speakers hissed a little, with noise that wandered in from the stars and stranger things than stars nature had set in this corner of the Galaxy.

Only a few hours earlier, in the middle of Waterfall's short autumn afternoon, there had been plenty to hear indeed. Driven by a priority code coming in advance of a vitally important message, the communicator had boomed itself to life, then roared the message through the house and across the entire base, in a voice that the four people heard plainly even four hundred meters distant where they were gathered to watch dolphins.

"*Sea Mother, this is Brass Trumpet. Predators here, and we're going to try to turn them. Hold your place. Repeating. . . .*"

One repetition of the substance came through, as the four were already hurrying back to the house. As soon as they got in they had played back the automatically recorded signal; and then when Glenna had at last located the code book somewhere, and they could verify the worst, they had played it back once more.

Sea Mother was the code name for any humans who might happen to be on Waterfall. It had been assigned by the military years ago, as part of their precautionary routine, and had probably never been used before today. Brass Trumpet, according to the book, was a name conveying a warning of deadly peril—it was to be used only by a human battle force when there were thought to be berserkers already in the Waterfall system or on their way to it. And "predators here" could hardly mean anything but berserkers—unliving and unmanned war machines, programmed to destroy whatever life they found. The first of them had been built in ages past, during the madness of some interstellar war between races now long-since vanished. Between berserkers and starfaring Earthhumans, war had now been chronic for a thousand standard years.

That Brass Trumpet's warning should be so brief and vague was understandable. The enemy would doubtless pick it up as soon as its intended hearers, and might well be able to decode it. But for all the message content revealed, Sea Mother might be another powerful human force, toward which Brass Trumpet sought to turn them. Or it would have been conceivable for such a message to be sent to no one, a planned deception to make the enemy waste computer capacity and detection instruments. And even if the berserkers' deadly electronic brains should somehow compute correctly that Sea Mother was a small and helpless target, it was still possible to hope that the berserkers would be too intent on fatter targets elsewhere, too hard-pressed by human forces, or both, to turn aside and snap up such a minor morsel.

During the hours since that first warning, there had come nothing but noise from the communicator. Glenna sighed, and reached out to pat her man on the arm below the sleeve of his loud shirt. "Busy day with the crustaceans tomorrow," she reminded him.

"So we'd better get some rest. I know." Ino looked and sounded worn. He was the only one of the four who had ever seen berserkers before, at anything like close range; and it was not exactly reassuring to see how grimly and intensely he reacted to the warning of their possible approach.

"You can connect the small alarm," Glenna went on, "so it'll be sure to wake us if another priority message comes in."

That, thought Claus, would be easier on the nerves than being blasted out of sleep by that God-voice shouting again, this time only a few meters from the head of their bed.

"Yes, I'll do that." Ino thought, then slapped his chair-arms. He made his voice a little brighter. "You're right about tomorrow. And over in Twenty-three we're going to have to start feeding the mantis shrimp." He glanced round at the wall near his chair, where a long chart showed ponds, bays, lagoons and tidal pools, all strung out in a kilometers-long array, most of it natural, along this part of the coast. This array was a chief reason why the Sea Mother base had been located where it was.

From its sun and moon to its gravity and atmosphere, Waterfall was remarkably Earthlike in almost every measurable attribute save one—this world was congenitally lifeless. About forty standard years past, during a lull in the seemingly interminable berserker-war, it had appeared that the peaceful advancement of interstellar humanization might get in an inning or two, and work had begun toward altering this lifelessness. Great ships had settled upon Waterfall with massive inoculations of Earthly life, in a program very carefully orchestrated to produce eventually a twin-Earth circling one of the few Sol-type suns in this part of the Galaxy.

The enormously complex task had been interrupted when war flared again. The first recrudescence of fighting was far away, but it drew off people and resources. A man-wife team of scientists were selected to stay alone on Waterfall for the duration of the emergency. They were to keep the program going along planned lines, even though at a slow pace. Ino and Glenna had been here for two years now. A supply ship from Atlantis called at intervals of a few standard months; and the last to call, eight local days ago, had brought along another husband-and-wife team for a visit. Claus and Jenny were both psychologists, interested in the study of couples living in isolation; and they were to stay at least until the next supply ship came.

So far the young guests had been welcome. Glenna, her own children long grown and independent on other worlds, approached motherliness sometimes in her attitude. Ino, more of a born competitor, swam races with Claus and gambled—lightly—with him. With Jenny he alternated between half-serious gallantry and teasing.

"I almost forgot," he said now, getting up from his chair before the communicator, and racking his arms and shoulders with an intense stretch. "I've got a little present for you, Jen."

"Oh?" She was bright, interested, imperturbable. It was her usual working attitude, which he persisted in trying to break through.

Ino went out briefly, and came back to join the others in the kitchen. A small snack before retiring had become a daily ritual for the group.

"For you," he said, presenting Jen with a small bag of clear plastic. There was water inside, and something else.

"Oh, my goodness." It was still her usual nurselike business tone, which evidently struck Ino as a challenge. "What do I do with it?"

"Keep him in that last aquarium in the parlor," Ino advised. "It's untenanted right now."

Claus, looking at the bag from halfway across the kitchen, made out in it one of those non-human, non-mammalian shapes that are apt to give Earth people the impression of the intensely alien, even when the organism sighted comes from their own planet. It was no bigger than an adult human finger, but replete with waving appendages. There came to mind something written by Lafcadio Hearn about a centipede: *The blur of its moving legs . . . toward which one would no more advance one's hand . . . than toward the spinning blade of a power saw . . .*

Or some words close to those. Jen, Claus knew, cared for the shapes of non-mammalian life even less than he did. But she would grit her teeth and struggle not to let the teasing old man see it.

"Just slit the bag and let it drain into the tank," Ino was advising, for once sounding pretty serious. "They don't like handling . . . okay? He's a bit groggy right now, but tomorrow, if he's not satisfied with you as his new owner, he may try to get away."

Glenna, in the background, was rolling her eyes in the general direction of Brass Trumpet, miming: What is the old fool up to now? When is he going to grow up?

"Get away?" Jen inquired sweetly. "You told me the other day that even a snail couldn't climb that glass—"

The house was filled with the insistent droning of the alarm that Ino had just connected. He's running some kind of test, Claus thought at once. Then he saw the other man's face and knew that Ino wasn't.

Already the new priority message was coming in: "*Sea Mother, the fight's over here. Predators departing Waterfall System. Repeating . . .*"

Claus started to obey an impulse to run out and look at the sky again, then realized that there would certainly be nothing to be seen of the battle now. Radio waves, no faster than light, had just announced that it was over. Instead he joined the others in voicing their mutual relief. They had a minute or so of totally unselfconscious cheering.

Ino, his face much relieved, broke out a bottle of something and four glasses. In a little while, all of them drifted noisily outside, unable to keep from looking up, though knowing they would find nothing but the stars to see.

"What," asked Claus, "were berserkers doing here in the first place? We're hardly a big enough target to be interesting to a fleet of them. Are we?"

"Not when they have bigger game in sight." Ino gestured upward with his drink. "Oh, any living target interests them, once they get it in their sights. But I'd guess that if a sizable force was here they were on the way to attack Atlantis. See, sometimes in space you can use a planet or a whole system as a kind of cover. Sneak up behind its solar wind, as it were, its gravitational vortex, as someone fighting a land war might take advantage of a mountain or a hill." Atlantis was a long-colonized system less than a dozen parsecs distant, heavily populated and heavily defended. The three habitable Atlantean planets were surfaced mostly with water, and the populace lived almost as much below the waves as on the shaky continents.

It was hours later when Glenna roused and stirred in darkness, pulling away for a moment from Ino's familiar angularity nestled beside her.

She blinked. "What was that?" she asked her husband, in a low voice barely cleared of sleep.

Ino scarcely moved. "What was what?"

"A flash, I thought. Some kind of bright flash, outside. Maybe in the distance."

There came no sound of thunder, or of rain. And no more flashes, either, in the short time Glenna remained awake.

Shortly after sunrise next morning, Claus and Jen went out for an early swim. Their beach, pointed out by their hosts as the place where swimmers would be safest and least likely to damage the new ecology, lay a few hundred meters along the shoreline to the west, with several tall dunes between it and the building complex.

As they rounded the first of these dunes, following the

pebbly shoreline, Claus stopped. "Look at that." A continuous track, suggesting the passage of some small, belly-dragging creature, had been drawn in the sand. Its lower extremity lay somewhere under water, its upper was concealed amid the humps of sterile sand somewhere inland.

"Something," said Jenny, "crawled up out of the water. I haven't seen that before on Waterfall."

"Or came down into it." Claus squatted beside the tiny trail. He was anything but a skilled tracker, and could see no way of determining which way it led. "I haven't seen anything like this before either. Glenna said certain species—I forget which—were starting to try the land. I expect this will interest them when we get back."

When Claus and Jenny had rounded the next dune, there came into view on its flank two more sets of tracks, looking very much like the first, and like the first either going up from the water or coming down.

"Maybe," Claus offered, "it's the same one little animal going back and forth. Do crabs make tracks like that?"

Jen couldn't tell him. "Anyway, let's hope they don't pinch swimmers." She slipped off her short robe and took a running dive into the cool water, whose salt content made it a good match for the seas of Earth. Half a minute later, she and her husband came to the surface together, ten meters or so out from shore. From here they could see west past the next dune. There, a hundred meters distant, underscored by the slanting shadows of the early sun, a whole tangled skein of narrow, fresh-looking tracks connected someplace inland with the sea.

A toss of Jen's head shook water from her long, dark hair. "I wonder if it's some kind of seasonal migration?"

"They certainly weren't there yesterday. I think I've had enough. This water's colder than a bureaucrat's heart."

Walking briskly, they had just re-entered the compound

when Jenny touched Claus on the arm. "There's Glenna, at the tractor shed. I'm going to trot over and tell her what we saw."

"All right. I'll fix some coffee."

Glenna, coming out of the shed a little distance inland from the main house, forestalled Jenny's announcement about the tracks with a vaguely worried question of her own.

"Did you or Claus see or hear anything strange last night, Jenny?"

"Strange? No, I don't think so."

Glenna looked toward a small cluster of more distant outbuildings. "We've just been out there taking a scheduled seismograph reading. It had recorded something rather violent and unusual, at about oh-two-hundred this morning. The thing is, you see, it must have been just about that time that something woke me up. I had the distinct impression that there had been a brilliant flash, somewhere outside."

Ino, also dressed in coveralls this morning, appeared among the distant sheds, trudging toward them. When he arrived, he provided more detail on the seismic event. "Quite sharp and apparently quite localized, not more than ten kilometers from here. Our system triangulated it well. I don't know when we've registered another event quite like it."

"What do you suppose it was?" Jen asked.

Ino hesitated minimally. "It could have been a very small spaceship crashing; or maybe a fairly large aircraft. But the only aircraft on Waterfall are the two little ones we have out in that far shed."

"A meteor, maybe?"

"I rather hope so. Otherwise a spacecraft just might be our most likely answer. And if it were a spacecraft from Brass Trumpet's force coming down here—crippled in the fighting, perhaps—we'd have heard from him on the subject, I should think.''

The remaining alternative hung in the air unvoiced. Jenny bit her lip. By now, Brass Trumpet must be long gone from the system, and impossible of recall, his ships outspacing light and radio waves alike in pursuit of the enemy force.

In a voice more worried than before, Glenna was saying: ''Of course if it was some enemy unit, damaged in the battle, then I suppose the crash is likely to have completed its destruction.''

''I'd better tell you,'' Jenny blurted in. And in a couple of sentences she described the peculiar tracks.

Ino stared at her with frank dismay. ''I was going to roll out an aircraft . . . but let me take a look at those tracks first.''

The quickest way to reach them was undoubtedly on foot, and the gnarled man trotted off along the beach path at such a pace that Jenny had difficulty keeping up. Glenna remained behind, saying she would let Claus know what was going on.

Moving with flashes of former athletic grace, Ino reached the nearest of the tracks and dropped to one knee beside it, just as Claus had done. ''Do the others look just like this?''

''As nearly as I could tell. We didn't get close to all of them.''

''That's no animal I ever saw.'' He was up again already, trotting back toward the base. ''I don't like it. Let's get airborne, all of us.''

''I always pictured berserkers as huge things.''

''Most of 'em are. Some are small machines, for specialized purposes.''

''I'll run into the house and tell the others to get ready to take off,'' Jenny volunteered as they sped into the compound.

''Do that. Glenna will know what to bring, I expect. I'll get a flyer rolled out of the shed.''

Running, Jen thought as she hurried into the house, gave substance to a danger that might otherwise have existed only in the mind. Could it be that Ino, with the horrors in his memory, was somewhat too easily alarmed where berserkers were concerned?

Glenna and Claus, who had just changed into coveralls, met her in the common room. She was telling them of Ino's decision to take to the air, and thinking to herself that she had better change out of her beach garb also, when the first outcry sounded from somewhere outside. It was less a scream than a baffled-sounding, hysterical laugh.

Glenna pushed past her at once, and in a moment was out the door and running. Exchanging a glance with her husband, Jenny turned and followed, Claus right at her heels.

The strange cry came again. Far ahead, past Glenna's running figure, the door of the aircraft shed had been slid back, and in its opening a white figure appeared outlined. A figure that reeled drunkenly and waved its arms.

Glenna turned aside at the tractor shed, where one of the small ground vehicles stood ready. They were used for riding, hauling, pushing sand, to sculpt a pond into a better shape or slice away part of a too-obtrusive dune. It'll be faster than running, Jenny thought, as she saw the older woman spring into the driver's seat, and heard the motor *whoosh* quietly to life. She leaped aboard too. Claus shoved strongly at her back to make sure she was safely on, before he used both hands for his own grip. A grip was necessary because they were already rolling, and accelerating quickly.

Ino's figure, now just outside the shed, came hurtling closer with their own speed. He shook his arms at them again and staggered. Upon his chest he wore a brownish thing the size of a small plate, like some great medallion that was so heavy it almost pulled him down. He clawed at the brown plate with both hands, and suddenly his coveralls in front were splashed with scarlet. He bellowed words which Jenny could not make out.

Claus gripped Glenna's shoulders and pointed. A dozen or more brown plates were scuttling on the brown, packed sand, between the aircraft shed and the onrushing tractor. The tracks they drew were faint replicas of those that had lined the softer sand along the beach. Beneath each saucer-like body, small legs blurred, reminding Claus of something recently seen, something he could not stop to think of now.

The things had nothing like the tractor's speed but still they were in position to cut it off. Glenna swerved no more than slightly, if at all, and one limbed plate disappeared beneath a wheel. It came up at once with the wheel's rapid turning, a brown blur seemingly embedded in the soft, fat tire, resisting somehow the centrifugal force that might have thrown it off.

Ino had gone down with, as Claus now saw, three of the things fastened on his body, but he somehow fought back to his feet just as the tractor jerked to a halt beside him. If Claus could have stopped to analyze his own mental state, he might have said he lacked the time to be afraid. With a blow of his fist he knocked one of the attacking things away from Ino, and felt the surprising weight and hardness of it as a sharp pang up through his wrist.

All three dragging together, they pulled Ino aboard; Glenna was back in the driver's seat at once. Claus kicked another attacker off, then threw open the lid of the tractor's toolbox. He grabbed the longest, heaviest metal tool displayed inside.

A swarm of attackers were between them and the aircraft shed; and the shadowed shape of a flyer, just inside, was spotted with them too. As Glenna gunned the engine, she turned the tractor at the same time, heading back toward the main building and the sea beyond. In the rear seat, Jenny held Ino. He bled on everything, and his eyes were fixed on the sky while his mouth worked in terror. In the front, Claus fought to protect the driver and himself.

A brown plate scuttled onto the cowling, moving for Glenna's hands on the controls. Claus swung, a baseball batter, bright metal blurring at the end of his extended arms. There was a hard, satisfying crunch, as of hard plastic or ceramic cracking through. The brown thing fell to the floor, and he caught a glimpse of dull limbs still in motion before he caught it with a foot and kicked it out onto the flying ground.

Another of the enemy popped out from somewhere onto the dash. He pounded at it, missed when it seemed to dodge his blows. He cracked its body finally; but still it clung on under the steering column, hard to get at, inching toward Glenna's fingers. Claus grabbed it with his left hand, felt a lance. Not until he had thrown the thing clear of the tractor did he look at his hand and see two fingers nearly severed.

At the same moment, the tractor engine died, and they were rolling to a silent stop, with the sea and the small dock Glenna had been steering for only a few meters ahead. Under the edge of the engine cowling another of the enemy appeared, thrusting forward a limb that looked like a pair of ceramic pliers, shredded electrical connectors dangling in its grip.

The humans abandoned the tractor in a wordless rush. Claus, one hand helpless and dripping blood, aided the women with Ino as best he could. Together they half-dragged, half-carried him across the dock and rolled him into a small, open boat, the only craft at once available. In moments Glenna had freed them from the dock and started the motor, and they were headed out away from shore.

Away from shore, but not into the sea. They were separated from deep-blue and choppy ocean by a barrier reef or causeway, one of the features that had made this coast desirable for life-seeding base. The reef, a basically natural structure of sand and rock deposited by waves and currents, was about a hundred meters from the shore, and stretched in either direction as far as vision carried. Running from beach to reef, artificial walls or low causeways of fused rock separated ponds of various sizes.

"We're in a kind of square lagoon here," Glenna told Jenny, motioning for her to take over the job of steering. "Head for that far corner. If we can get there ahead of them, we may be able to lift the boat over the reef and get out."

Jen nodded, taking the controls. Glenna slid back to a place beside her husband, snapped open the boat's small first-aid kit, and began applying pressure bandages.

Claus started to try to help, saw the world beginning to turn gray around him, and slumped back against the gunwale; no use to anyone if he passed out. Ino looked as if he had been attacked, not by teeth or claws or knives, but by several sets of nail-pullers and wire-cutters. His chest still rose and fell, but his eyes were closed now and he was gray with shock. Glenna draped a thermal blanket over him.

Jen was steering around the rounded structure, not much bigger than a phone booth, protruding above the water in the middle of the pond. Most of the ponds and bays had similar observation stations. Claus had looked into one or two and he thought now that there was nothing in them likely to be of any help. More first-aid kits, perhaps— but what Ino needed was the big medirobot back at the house.

And he was not going to get it. By now the building complex must be overrun by the attackers. Berserkers . . .

"Where can we find weapons?" Claus croaked at Glenna.

"Let's see that hand. I can't do any more for Ino now . . . I'll bandage this. If you mean guns, there are a couple at the house, somewhere in storage. We can't go back there now."

"I know."

Glenna had just let go his hand when from the front seat there came a scream. Claws and a brown saucer-shape were climbing in over the gunwale at Jenny's side. Had the damned thing come aboard somehow with them, from the tractor? Or was this pond infested with them too?

In his effort to help drag Ino to the boat, Claus had abandoned his trusty wrench beside the tractor. He grabbed now for the best substitute at hand, a small anchor at the end of a chain. His overhand swing missed Jenny's head by less than he had planned, but struck the monster like a mace. It fell into the bottom of the boat, vibrating its limbs, as Claus thought, uselessly; then he realized that it was making a neat hole.

His second desperation-swing came down upon it squarely. One sharp prong of the anchor broke a segment of the brown casing clean away, and something sparked and sizzled when the sea came rushing in—

—seawater rushing—

—into the bottom of the boat—

The striking anchor had enlarged the hole that the enemy had begun. The bottom was split, the boat was taking water fast.

Someone grabbed up the sparking berserker, inert now save for internal fireworks, and hurled it over the side. Glenna threw herself forward, taking back the wheel, and Jenny scrambled aft, to help one-handed Claus with bailing.

The boat limped, staggered, gulped water and wallowed

on toward the landbar. It might get them that far, but forget the tantalizing freedom of blue surf beyond . . .

Jenny started to say something to her husband, then almost shrieked again, as Ino's hand, resurgently alive, came up to catch her wrist. The old man's eyes were fixed on hers with a tremendous purpose. He gasped out words, and then fell back unable to do more.

The words first registered with Jenny as: ". . . need them . . . do the splashers . . ." It made no sense.

Glenna looked back briefly, then had to concentrate on boathandling. In another moment the fractured bottom was grating over rock. Claus scrambled out and held the prow against the above-water portion of the reef. The women followed, got their footing established outside the boat, then turned to lift at Ino's inert form.

Jenny paused. "Glenna, I'm afraid he's gone."

"No!" Denial was fierce and absolute. "Help me!"

Jen almost started to argue, then gave in. They got Ino up into a fireman's-carry position on Claus's shoulders; even with a bad hand he was considerably stronger than either of the women. Then the three began to walk east along the reef. At high tide, as now, it was a strip of land no more than three or four meters wide, its low crest half a meter above the water. Waves of any size broke over it. Fortunately today the surf was almost calm.

Claus could feel the back of his coverall and neck wetting with Ino's blood. He shifted the dead weight on his shoulders. All right, so far. But his free hand, mutilated, throbbed.

He asked: "How far are we going, Glenna?"

"I don't know." The woman paced ahead—afraid to look at her husband now?—staring into the distance. "There isn't any place. Keep going."

Jenny and Claus exchanged looks. For want of any better plan at the moment, they kept going. Jen took a look back. "They're on the reef, and on the shore too, following us. A good distance back."

Claus looked, and looked again a minute later. Brown speckles by the dozen followed, but were not catching up. Not yet.

Now they were passing the barrier of fused rock separating the pond in which they had abandoned the boat from its neighbor. The enemy moving along the shore would intercept them, or very nearly, if they tried to walk the barrier back to land.

Ahead, the reef still stretched interminably into a sun-dazzled nothingness.

"What's in this next pond, Glenna?" Claus asked, and knew a measure of relief when the gray-haired woman gave a little shake of her head and answered sensibly.

"Grouper. Some other fish as food stock for them. Why?"

"Just wondering. What'll we run into if we keep on going in this direction?"

"This just goes on. Kilometer after kilometer. Ponds, and bays, and observation stations—I say keep going because otherwise they'll catch us. What do you think we ought to do?"

Claus abruptly stopped walking, startling the women. He let the dead man slide down gently from his shoulders. Jen looked at her husband, examined Ino, shook her head.

Claus said: "I think we've got to leave him."

Glenna looked down at Ino's body once, could not keep looking at him. She nodded fiercely, and once more led the way.

A time of silent walking passed before Jenny at Claus's side began: "If they're berserkers . . ."

"What else?"

"Well, why aren't we all dead already? They don't seem very . . . efficiently designed for killing."

"They must be specialists," Claus mused. "Only a small part of a large force, a part Brass Trumpet missed when the rest moved on or was destroyed. Remember, we were wondering if Atlantis was their real target? These are special machines, built for . . . underwater work, maybe. Their ship must have been wrecked in the fighting and had to come down. When they found themselves on this planet they must have come down to the sea for a reconnaissance, and then decided to attack first by land. Probably they saw the lights of the base before they crash-landed. They know which life-form they have to deal with first, on any planet. Not very efficient, as you say. But they'll keep coming at us till they're all smashed or we're all dead."

Glenna had slowed her pace a little and was looking toward the small observation post rising in the midst of the pond that they were passing. "I don't think there's anything in any of these stations that can help us. But I can't think of anywhere else to turn."

Claus asked: "What's in the next pond after this?"

"Sharks . . . ah. That might be worth a try. Sometimes they'll snap at anything that moves. They're small ones, so I think our risk will be relatively small if we wade out to the middle."

Claus thought to himself that he would rather end in the belly of a live shark than be torn to pieces by an impersonal device. Jen was willing also to take the chance.

They did not pause again till they were on the brink of the shark pond. Then Glenna said: "The water will be no more than three or four feet deep the way we're going. Stay together and keep splashing as we go. Claus, hold that bad hand up; mustn't drip a taste of blood into the water."

And in they went. Only when they were already splashing waist-deep did Claus recall Ino's blood wetting the back of his coverall. But he was not going to stop just now to take it off.

The pond was not very large; a minute of industrious wading, and they were climbing unmolested over the low, solid railing of the observation post rising near its middle. Here was space for two people to sit comfortably, sheltered from weather by a transparent dome and movable side panels. In the central console were instruments that continually monitored the life in the surrounding pond. Usually, of course, the readings from all ponds would be monitored in the more convenient central station attached to the house.

The three of them squeezed in, and Glenna promptly opened a small storage locker. It contained a writing instrument that looked broken, a cap perhaps left behind by some construction worker, and a small spider—another immigrant from Earth, of course—who might have been blown out here by the wind. That was all.

She slammed the locker shut again. "No help. So now it's a matter of waiting. They'll obviously come after us through the water. The sharks may snap up some of them before they reach us. Then we must be ready to move on before we are surrounded. It's doubtful, and risky, but I can't think of anything else to try."

Claus frowned. "Eventually we'll have to circle around, get back to the buildings."

Jen frowned at him. "The berserkers are there, too."

"I don't think they will be, now. You see—"

Glenna broke in: "Here they come."

The sun had climbed, and was starting to get noticeably hot. It came to Claus's mind, not for the first time since their flight had started, that there was no water for them to drink. He held his left arm up with his right, trying to ease the throbbing.

Along the reef where they had walked, along the parallel shore—and coming now over the barrier from the grouper pond—plate-sized specks of brown death were flowing. There were several dozen of them, moving more slowly than hurried humans could move, almost invisible in the shimmer of sun and sea. Some plopped into the water of the shark pond as Claus watched.

"I can't pick them up underwater," Glenna announced. She was twiddling the controls of the station's instruments, trying to catch the enemy on one of the screens meant for observing marine life. "Sonar . . . motion detectors . . . water's too murky for simple video."

Understanding dawned for Claus. "That's why they're not metal! Why they're comparatively fragile. They're designed for avoiding detection by underwater defenses, on Atlantis I suppose, for infiltrating and disabling them."

Jen was standing. "We'd better get moving before we're cut off."

"In another minute." Glenna was still switching from one video pickup to another around the pond. "I'm sure we have at least that much to spare . . . ah."

One of the enemy had appeared on screen, sculling toward the camera at a modest pace. It looked less lifelike than it had in earlier moments of arm's-length combat.

Now, entering the picture from the rear, a shark.

Claus was not especially good on distinguishing marine species. But this portentous and somehow familiar shape was identifiable at once, not to be confused even by the non-expert, it seemed, with that of any other kind of fish.

Claus started to say, He's going right past. But the shark was not. Giving the impression of afterthought, the torpedo-shape swerved back. Its mouth opened and the berserker device was gone.

The people watching made wordless sounds. But Jen took the others by an arm apiece. "We can't bet all of them will be eaten—let's get moving."

Claus already had one leg over the station's low railing when the still surface of the pond west of the observation post exploded. Leaping clear of the water, the premier killer of Earth's oceans twisted in mid-air, as if trying to snap at its own belly. It fell back, vanishing in a hill of lashed-up foam. A moment later it jumped again, still thrashing.

In the fraction of a second when the animal was clearly visible, Claus watched the dark line come into being across its white belly as if traced there by an invisible pen. It was a short line that a moment later broadened and evolved in blood. As the fish rolled on its back something dark and pointed came into sight, spreading the edges of the hole. Then the convulsing body of the shark had vanished, in an eruption of water turned opaque with its blood.

The women were wading quickly away from the platform in the opposite direction, calling him to follow, hoping aloud that the remaining sharks would be drawn to the dying one. But for one moment longer Claus lingered, staring at the screen. It showed the roiling bloody turmoil of killer fish converging, and out of this cloud the little berserker emerged, unfazed by shark's teeth or digestion, resuming its methodical progress toward the humans, the life-units that could be really dangerous to the cause of death.

Jen tugged at her husband, got him moving with them. In her exhausted brain a nonsense-rhyme was being generated: *Bloody water hides the slasher, seed them, heed them, sue the splashers . . .*

No!

As the three completed their water-plowing dash to the east edge of the pond, and climbed out, Jenny took Glenna by the arm. "Something just came to me. When I was tending Ino—he said something before he died."

They were walking east along the barrier reef again. "He said smashers," Jen continued. "That was it. Lead them or feed them, to the smashers. But I still don't understand—"

Glenna stared at her for a moment, an almost frightening gaze. Then she stepped between the young couple and pulled them forward.

Two ponds down she turned aside, wading through water that splashed no higher than their calves, directly toward another observation post that looked just like the last.

"We won't be bothered in here," she assured them. "We're too big. Of course, of course. Oh, Ino. I should have thought of this myself. Unless we should happen to step right on one, but there's very little chance of that. They wait in ambush most of the time, in holes or under rocks."

"They?" Injury and effort were taking toll on Claus. He leaned on Jenny's shoulder now.

Glenna glanced back impatiently. "Mantis shrimp is the common name. They're stomatopods, actually."

"Shrimp?" The dazed query was so soft that she may not have heard it.

A minute later they were squeezed aboard the station and could rest again. Above, clean morning clouds were building to enormous height, clouds that might have formed in the unbreathed air of Earth five hundred million years before.

"Claus," Jen asked, when both of them had caught their breath a little, "what were you saying a while ago, about circling back to the house?"

"It's this way," he said, and paused to organize his thoughts. "We've been running to nowhere, because there's nowhere on this world we can get help. *But the berserkers can't know that.* I'm assuming they haven't scouted the whole planet, but just crash-landed on it. For all they know, there's another colony of humans just down the coast. Maybe a town, with lots of people, aircraft, weapons . . . so for them it's an absolute priority to cut us off before we can give a warning. Therefore every one of their units must be committed to the chase. And if we can once get through them or around them, we can outrun them home, to vehicles and guns and food and water. How we get through them or around them I haven't figured out yet. But I don't see any other way.''

"We'll see," said Glenna. Jen held his hand, and looked at him as if his idea might be reasonable. A distracting raindrop hit him on the face, and suddenly a shower was spattering the pond. With open mouths the three survivors caught what drops they could. They tried spreading Jenny's robe out to catch more, but the rain stopped before the cloth was wet.

"Here they come," Glenna informed them, shading her eyes from re-emergent sun. She started tuning up the observing gear aboard the station.

Claus counted brown saucer-shapes dropping into the pond. Only nineteen, after all.

"Again, I can't find them with the sonar," Glenna muttered. "We'll try the television—there."

A berserker unit—for all the watching humans could tell, it was the same one that the shark had swallowed— was centimetering its tireless way toward them, walking the bottom in shallow, sunlit water. Death was walking. A living thing might run more quickly, for a time, but life would tire. Or let life oppose it, if life would. Already it had walked through a shark, as easily as traversing a mass of seaweed.

"There," Glenna breathed again. The advancing enemy had detoured slightly around a rock, and a moment later a dancing ripple of movement had emerged from hiding somewhere to follow in its path. The pursuer's score or so of tiny legs supported in flowing motion a soft-looking, roughly segmented tubular body. Its sinuous length was about the same as the enemy machine's diameter, but in

contrast the follower was aglow with life, gold marked in
detail with red and green and brown, like banners carried
forward above an advancing column. Long antennae waved
as if for balance above bulbous, short-stalked eyes. And
underneath the eyes a coil of heavy forelimbs rested, not
used for locomotion.

"*Odonodactylus syllarus*," Glenna murmured. "Not the
biggest species—but maybe big enough."

"What are they?" Jen's voice was a prayerful whisper.

"Well, predators . . ."

The berserker, intent on its own prey, ignored the ani-
mate ripple that was overtaking it, until the smasher had
closed almost to contact range. The machine paused then,
and started to turn.

Before it had rotated itself more than halfway its brown
body was visibly jerked forward, under some striking impetus from the smasher too fast for human eyes to follow.
The *krak!* of it came clearly through the audio pickup.
Even before the berserker had regained its balance, it put
forth a tearing-claw like that which had opened the shark's
gut from inside.

Again the invisible impact flicked from a finger-length
away. At each spot where one of the berserker's feet
touched bottom, a tiny spurt of sand jumped up with the
transmitted shock. Its tearing claw now dangled uselessly,
hard ceramic cracked clean across.

"I've never measured a faster movement by anything
that lives. They strike with special dactyls—well, with
their elbows, you might say. They feed primarily on hard-
shelled crabs and clams and snails. That was just a little
one, that Ino gave you as a joke. One as long as my hand
can hit something like a four-millimeter bullet—and some
of these are longer."

Another hungry smasher was now coming swift upon
the track of the brown, shelled thing that looked so like a

crab. The second smasher's eyes moved on their stalks, calculating distance. It was evidently of a different species than the first, being somewhat larger and of a variant coloration. Even as the berserker, which had just put out another tool, sharp and wiry, and cut its first assailant neatly in half, turned back, Claus saw—or almost saw or imagined that he saw—the newcomer's longest pair of forelimbs unfold and return. Again grains of sand beneath the two bodies, living and unliving, jumped from the bottom. With the concussion white radii of fracture sprang out across a hard, brown surface . . .

Four minutes later the three humans were still watching, in near-perfect silence. A steady barrage of *kraks*, from every region of the pond, were echoing through the audio pickups. The video screen still showed the progress of the first individual combat.

"People sometimes talk about sharks as being aggressive, as terrible killing machines. Gram for gram, I don't think they're at all in the same class."

The smashing stomatopod, incongruously shrimplike, gripping with its six barb-studded smaller forelimbs the ruined casing of its victim—from which a single ceramic walking-limb still thrashed—began to drag it back to the rock from which its ambush had been launched. Once there, it propped the interstellar terror in place, a Lilliputian monster blacksmith arranging metal against anvil. At the next strike, imaginable if not visible as a double backhand snap from the fists of a karate master, fragments of tough casing literally flew through the water, mixed now with a spill of delicate components. What, no soft, delicious meat in sight as yet? Then *smash* again . . .

An hour after the audio pickups had reported their last *krak*, the three humans walked toward home, unmolested through the shallows and along a shore where no brown saucers moved.

When Ino had been brought home, and Claus's hand seen to, the house was searched for enemy survivors. Guns were got out, and the great gates in the sand-walls closed to be on the safe side. Then the two young people sent Glenna to a sedated rest.

Her voice was dazed, and softly, infinitely tired. "Tomorrow we'll feed them, something real."

"This afternoon," said Claus. "When you wake up. Show me what to do."

"Look at this," called Jen a minute later, from the common room.

One wall of the smallest aquarium had been shattered outward. Its tough glass lay sharded on the carpet, along with a large stain of water and the soft body of a small creature, escaped and dead.

Jen picked it up. It was much smaller than its cousins out in the pond, but now she could not mistake the shape, even curled loosely in her palm.

Her husband came in and looked over her shoulder. "Glenna's still muttering. She just told me they can stab, too, if they sense soft meat in contact. Spear-tips on their smashers when they unfold them all the way. So you couldn't hold him like that if he was still alive." Claus's voice broke suddenly, in a delayed reaction.

"Oh, yes I could." Jen's voice too. "Oh, yes I could indeed."